THE MYSTERY OF THE CURIOSITIES

SNOW & WINTER: BOOK TWO

C.S. POE

This is a work of fiction. Names, characters, places, and incidents either are the product of the author's imagination or are used fictitiously, and any resemblance to actual persons, living or dead, business establishments, events, or locales is entirely coincidental.

The Mystery of the Curiosities
Copyright © 2017, 2020 by C.S. Poe

All rights reserved. No part of this book may be reproduced in any form, stored in any retrieval system, or transmitted in any form by any means—electronic, mechanical, photocopy, recording, or otherwise—without prior written permission of the publisher, except as provided by United States of America copyright law. For permission requests and all other inquiries, contact: contact@cspoe.com

Published by Emporium Press
https://www.cspoe.com
contact@cspoe.com

Cover Art by Reese Dante
Cover content is for illustrative purposes only and any person depicted on the cover is a model.

Published 2020.
First Edition published 2017. Second Edition 2020.
Printed in the United States of America

Trade Paperback ISBN: 978-1-952133-02-2
Digital eBook ISBN: 978-1-952133-03-9

For Megan.
My best friend and Sebastian's first fan.

CHAPTER ONE

Tuesday morning began with a brick through the Emporium window.

The seconds that followed were strangely silent. Nothing but the gentle patter of frozen February rain. Then my heart remembered to keep beating, and I could hear its *thud, thud, thud* in my ears. A few pieces of glass cracked from the top of the large bay window frame and fell to the wooden floor. The sound of New York City traffic invaded my quiet, cozy cave of a shop.

"What the fuck!" Max shouted. He moved to run by me at the counter, but I grabbed his shoulders.

"Be careful," I said, pointing at the ceramic coffee mug I'd dropped when the shattered glass scared the ever-loving hell out of me.

Max jumped over the mess and down the steps from the register. He motioned wildly at the window. "What the fuck?" he declared again.

I'll say.

I walked down the stairs and studied the scene. Glass was everywhere and rain was coming in. "Grab a trash bag from the office."

"The glass will just slice——"

"To put over the displays before they get soaked. Go."

Max ran to get the bags.

I pinched the bridge of my nose and took a deep breath. What a way to start the week.

Pushing my glasses up, I went to the door, threw it open, and stepped out into the miserable morning. Rain splattered my lenses and dampened my sweater. My breath puffed around me while I looked up and down the sidewalk, as if I'd find the vandal hanging out and waiting to be caught. A couple paying the meter nearby were looking at the window in horror, and a man walking his tiny dog had to pick the animal up to avoid glass on the sidewalk.

Max was spreading out trash bags on nearby displays. "Did someone spray-paint a dick on the door too?" he called.

"No," I answered before going back inside. "Why?"

"Add insult to injury. Should I move this stuff away from the window?"

I tugged my phone from my back pocket. "Hold on. Let me get some pictures before we move anything." I snapped photos of the window and floor before motioning him to continue.

When I stepped away from the immediate area, I noticed the brick across the room. I went over, crouched down, and picked it up. It was just an ordinary brick. With a rubber band wrapped around it. I set my phone on the floor beside me and turned it around to see a folded piece of wet paper on the other side.

Hell. There were easier ways to get in touch with me. There was this great invention called the telephone.

Even a carrier pigeon would have been better. Because a pigeon would just crap on my inventory and be gone. A pigeon didn't require a police report, insurance paperwork, and my jerk of a landlord coming down to inspect this mess.

I yanked the rubber band free and unfolded the paper. I don't know what I had been expecting as I held it close to read, but it wasn't *I know you like mysteries*.

"What're you doing?" Max asked.

I glanced over my shoulder. "Someone attached a note to the brick."

"What does it say?"

"'I know you like mysteries.'"

"Me?"

"No, that's what the note says," I replied while waving the paper over my shoulder. I picked up my phone again and stood, knees cracking like I was an old man and not just a crabby thirty-three-year-old. I turned around and saw Max had gone very still. "Are you okay?"

"This isn't going to be like Christmas, is it?"

Duncan Andrews had thoroughly fucked up my holidays. He'd been responsible for the death of my former boss, had harassed and stalked me, and had shot Detective Calvin Winter.

"No," I said firmly, shaking my head. "Duncan is rocking an orange jumpsuit now."

"What about a copycat?"

"Poe never hurled bricks into antique shops. It's okay, really."

I told Max to finish with the displays and gave the police a ring to report the vandalism. Two officers arrived after I had gotten off the phone with Luther North, my landlord, who gave me more than an earful about the window, as if I had been asking for punks to hurl bricks at it.

"Do you have insurance, Mr. Snow?" the male officer asked. He'd introduced himself as Officer Lowry and had uncomfortably reminded me of Neil: same build and hair, same strong face and handsome features. But thankfully, there was no relation.

"Yeah. And the landlord is on his way now," I answered. A cold breeze blew in through the gaping window, and I shivered while crossing my arms over my chest.

The woman officer smiled and pointed at me. "I was here two months ago."

"I'm sorry?"

"When there was a pig's heart in your floor."

"Oh." I nodded and had to resist the urge to look over my shoulder at the spot in question. "No dismembered body parts this time."

She laughed quietly. "That's good."

Lowry, who had been writing notes, asked me a few more questions. Did I have any disgruntled customers lately? Had I received threats prior? But no. The entire event seemed completely unprovoked. To the point that I had considered someone threw the brick through the wrong window.

Except….

I know you like mysteries.

"Wait, before I forget," I said suddenly. "There was a note wrapped around the brick." I pulled the folded paper from the pocket of my sweater. "Here."

The female officer accepted the note. "Does this mean anything to you?"

I shrugged. "Not really. Unless the person who broke

my window is judging me for my reading habits."

Among other things.

She handed it back. "We'll see if any businesses across the street have surveillance videos we can look over, but you should know that the chances of catching who did this are very slim."

"I figured," I replied. "Worth a shot, though."

Luther walked into the shop as the officers left. He spoke with them briefly at the door before working his way through the cramped aisles toward me. His big belly pushed objects around on their displays as he moved through, and Max came up behind him to fix everything.

"Sebastian," Luther said with a bit of a wheeze. "What happened?"

"Exactly as I said on the phone, Mr. North. Someone threw a brick through the window."

"Why?" he asked, yanking a wadded pile of tissues from his coat pocket to dab his face.

"I didn't think to ask them," I answered.

"There you go with those smart-aleck responses. And before this, it was that creepy queer kid! He's in jail now, right?"

"Yup."

Luther paused from wiping his face. "Er—no offense with the queer thing."

"My fragile ego is still intact. Mr. North, it's currently raining in my store. How soon can this window be fixed?"

"Oh, well! It's simply not that easy, Sebastian! I have to file a claim with the property insurance."

"Which they'll pay. Vandalism by an unknown assailant isn't worth their time to investigate."

"Yes, but it still takes a few days."

"It's raining in here," I stated again, in case he

hadn't noticed.

"I can get a tarp."

"Not exactly going to keep the riffraff out."

"That's why stores have metal gates," Luther pointed out, as if I were dense.

"That's fine. But I have books in here that are worth up to five grand. If they get warped or damaged—"

"I'll have my boys come down and put up some sheets of plywood," Luther growled. "Happy?"

"I'll be happy when I have a new window."

I didn't want to spend the day cleaning up broken glass, wiping down and checking antiques that had gotten wet, and listening to the sexy voice of Frank Sinatra get drowned out by three of Luther's construction guys nailing plywood over the empty window frame, but I did. And I wasn't pleased about it. Leaving the shop for the night with such *bulletproof* security made me nervous.

Not that I could be blamed.

Explaining to Luther just how much my inventory was worth caused him to stay behind and personally oversee his workers.

I guess I should have been flattered.

But frankly, by the time I got home, kicked off my shoes, and dropped my coat on the floor while heading for the kitchen, I was tired. And cranky. I had a headache that was still in sync with the echo of hammers. I popped off the cap to a beer bottle and took a swig. I tugged a take-out menu free from under a fridge magnet, brought it closer to read, and took another sip. I had gotten as far as sweet-and-sour chicken and was deciding over dumplings or fried rice as a too-greasy side dish when there was a knock at the door. I raised my head and listened. I heard a key push into the lock and the door get nudged open.

Thank Christ.

I stepped out of the kitchen. "Hey. You're a sight for sore eyes."

Calvin smiled as he shut and locked the door behind him. "Did you just get home?"

"Few minutes ago. I thought you couldn't make it tonight?"

"Want me to go?" he countered.

"Don't even try."

Calvin tugged off his coat and hung it up. "How was your day?" he asked, walking across the room toward me. He took my face into his big hands, leaned down, and kissed my mouth.

"Better now," I murmured, kissing him again. "Catch any bad guys?"

"Sure did." Calvin threaded his fingers through my hair. "You okay?"

"Headache. I just listened to the Hammer Symphony in E Minor for the last hour."

"Come again?"

"Someone broke one of my windows today."

"You're kidding."

I shook my head. "Nope. Threw a brick through it. My landlord had some plywood put up. It's really classy."

Calvin moved his hands to squeeze my shoulders. "Sorry to hear that, baby."

"It's fine. Worse things have happened." I tugged him down by his tie. "Come here. I'm not done with you yet."

A smile crossed his face once more, and his warm mouth touched mine. Calvin tasted like *home*, if home were his trademark flavors of coffee and cinnamon mints and male, at least. I hadn't seen him in a few days, and I starved for him when we were apart. Nothing could fill that emptiness but Calvin himself.

We had officially started dating just before the New Year. It was both terrifying and perfect.

He was perfect.

I pushed his suit coat open and tugged it from his shoulders. Calvin helped, tossing it onto the couch. He broke away long enough to unbuckle his shoulder holster and take his weapon off. Setting it aside with his coat, Calvin then grabbed the back of my head, pulling me into another hot and heavy kiss.

My stomach growled loudly.

I stilled, and Calvin laughed against my mouth.

"Shut up," I muttered.

He grinned and stroked my cheek. "Let's eat first."

My face felt flushed as I took a step back. "The needs of my stomach aren't as strong as the needs of my dick."

"I believe you," Calvin said as he moved by and walked into the kitchen. "Chinese?"

Damn it. If Calvin hadn't eaten today, as he was prone to doing while working, I'd definitely lost my chance at a quickie.

"Did you eat?" I asked, following him back to the kitchen.

"Not yet."

Calvin was staring at the open menu when I walked in. I leaned against the doorframe, hands in my pockets, studying him. Even though we'd been together for a month and a half, this was still surreal as hell. Sometimes I thought my vision was getting worse, and I'd watch him extra hard, as if to be sure he wasn't a trick of the eye that would slowly dissipate.

But Calvin was real.

Real and breathing and *mine.*

When I first met Calvin, it was frightening to come to the realization that he was my soul mate. It was a nightmare when the world around us seemed insistent that we would never be an item. It had broken my heart, frankly. It's pretty fucking melodramatic, but there was a brief moment last year when I didn't know how I would live without loving Calvin.

A bullet really changes things. It makes you realize how short and precious life actually is.

And it gave Calvin the courage to come out at his age. To his family, who had all but locked him out of their homes and hearts, to his partner, Quinn Lancaster, to my dad, and to the world in general, really. And I know it must have scared him.

But he did it for *us.*

"Are you staring at me?" Calvin asked, not looking up from the list of food.

I blinked and straightened. "Sure am."

"Why's that?"

"You're pretty."

He snorted and glanced at me. "I'll order. What do you want?" Calvin pulled his phone out.

"Sweet-and-sour chicken." I walked into the kitchen and wrapped my arms around him from behind, resting my forehead against his back as I listened to Calvin call the restaurant and place our order for delivery. "I hope my fortune cookie says I get lucky tonight," I said as he hung up.

Calvin laughed as he put his phone away. "I wouldn't worry too much about what the cookie says."

For how shitty the day started, it certainly ended on

a high note: cheap food, a few beers, and classic Buster Keaton films on the couch with Calvin. I liked old black-and-white movies. They were easier to watch, what with never being overwhelmed by the mess of tones and colors blending into one another that represented modern cinema. Plus, silent films were underappreciated. Keaton was by far more brilliant than most of today's actors, and I don't care how old and crotchety that statement makes me sound. I sat cross-legged, cardboard container balanced on my knee. Snapping a pair of chopsticks apart, I dug into dinner.

"What's this one called?" Calvin asked, pointing at the screen.

"*Sherlock Jr.*," I said between bites. "One of my favorites."

"It would be."

"Don't tease."

Calvin laughed quietly. He took a few bites of his food, which really meant he cleaned out half of the container, before asking, "So what happened with the brick?"

"The brick," I muttered in annoyance. "Some asshole failed to recognize that I have a telephone."

"What?"

I waved the chopsticks in my hand while finishing the bite I'd just taken. "Sorry. There was a note attached to the brick." I turned to look at Calvin in the dim light, realizing I had his full and undivided attention. "Uh-oh."

"Uh-oh?" he repeated.

"You went from Calvin to Detective Winter real fast."

He frowned. "What did the note say?"

I leaned over to set the takeout on the coffee table before pulling the folded note out again. I opened it and handed it over. "'I know you like mysteries.'"

Calvin took the paper, narrowing his eyes as he looked it over. "I'm assuming you filed a police report?"

"Yup."

"Did you tell them about this?"

"Yeah. They didn't really seem to think much of it."

Calvin handed it back. "Sounds personal."

"I guess." I set the note on the coffee table before turning to Calvin. "But what am I supposed to make of it? I read Christopher Holmes's mysteries, so sue me."

"And Christie, Doyle, English—"

"All right, all right. I read a lot of mysteries. I get it."

Calvin put a hand on my knee. "Nothing else out of the ordinary has happened?"

"No." I put my hand over his, running my fingertips along his knuckles. "Max brought up an interesting point, though."

"What's that?"

"A copycat."

Calvin slowly shook his head. "No, I don't believe that's the case. A copycat tries to emulate the original criminal, so he or she wouldn't have acknowledged you in such a forward fashion in this case. Andrews couldn't rationalize the world outside of Poe's writing. I'd suspect anyone else attempting to pick up where he left off would at least reproduce his form of communication."

"That's more or less what I figured," I replied. "Still. It's weird."

"I'll make some calls tomorrow," Calvin said. "Check in and see if he's had any visitors."

"Thanks. I appreciate that."

"Of course, sweetie." Calvin resumed eating again

before he asked, "Promise me one thing?"

I leaned over to grab my food from the table, but paused and looked sideways at Calvin. "What's that?"

"You won't take it upon yourself to investigate, if something else were to happen."

"Very funny," I muttered, taking my carton.

"I'm being serious, Seb."

"I'm well aware of who the detective is in this relationship."

Calvin grunted.

The only murders I was trying to solve these days were in the paperbacks I'd read a dozen times already. I admit that hunting for clues and piecing a real-life mystery together was a thrill I could easily become addicted to, but in the end, I wasn't one for violence. The thought of firing another gun in my lifetime was more than enough to rein me in.

We all have our strengths and should stick to what best suits us. Calvin was made to fight bad guys. It was in his DNA to be a hero, to save people, to solve crimes. Me? I'm a hoarder of information. I know the history of picture buttons and of Victorian mourning clothes. I know how to spot fake tin types. And I liked what I did.

Antiques suited my temperament just fine.

Besides. Solving crimes Calvin-style meant being extremely fit, and I was more of the second-slice-of-cake sort of guy.

After *Sherlock Jr.*, we watched Buster Keaton's *Cops*, which got quite a number of laughs from Calvin. We were about halfway through *Steamboat Bill, Jr.* when the effects of greasy food, beers, and a dark room began to get the best of me. I felt Calvin pet my head and I opened my eyes.

"Want to go to bed?"

"Did I fall asleep?" I asked in return, yawning.

"Dozed off."

I blinked a few times and sat up from where I had been leaning against Calvin's shoulder. The sound of heavy rain could be heard over the slapstick music.

Calvin reached for the remote and turned the film off. "Come on."

I nodded, got to my feet, and went into the bathroom to brush my teeth and take out my contacts. When I came out again, Calvin had already turned off the lights and locked up for the night. I went into my bedroom and changed for bed while he took his turn in the bathroom.

We definitely weren't living together, but Calvin did prefer to spend what little time he had at my place instead of vice versa. My apartment was bigger, for one, but I think, more importantly, it had a homey feel. My place was well lived-in, whereas Calvin's felt like a glorified hotel room. And because he tried to spend at least an evening or two a week with me, a few extra garments had found their way into my closet.

It was always a bit exciting to see one of his suits hung up beside my crappy sweaters. It was an ever-present reminder that Calvin wasn't a vivid hallucination. He was real, he was wonderful, and he wanted to be with *me*.

I yawned again, plugging my phone into the charger and beginning to set the alarm clock when Calvin walked in. I glanced over, watching as he unbuttoned his shirt and dropped it into my dirty laundry. Strong muscles flexed as he continued undressing, and I realized it'd been nearly a week since I'd gotten to dig my fingers into his back and arms.

Calvin sat on the right side of the bed—his side—before leaning over and kissing the back of my neck. "Lay down," he whispered.

"What time do you need to be up?" I countered, hand still on the alarm clock.

"Worry about it later," Calvin said, trailing a hand down my back and under the ratty T-shirt I'd thrown on.

"Copy that, Major," I answered, hastily setting my glasses aside and turning to face him.

He rolled onto his back, wrapped a hand around my neck, and tugged me toward him. I climbed on top, legs on either side of Calvin's hips, and leaned down to kiss his mouth. I moved my hands up and down his bare chest, fingertips practically buzzing as they caressed warm skin and hair. Calvin's own hands moved along my back as he kissed me, then slid down to cup my ass.

"I want to suck your cock," Calvin growled.

"Yeah?" I whispered.

He grinned against my mouth. "Yeah, baby. Come up here."

I nodded and sat up, letting Calvin help me out of my pajama pants and toss them somewhere in the dark. I moved to rest my knees on either side of Calvin's chest, leaning over him. "Like this?"

He hummed in contentment, reaching up to stroke me slowly. "Look at how big and beautiful. I want your entire dick down my throat."

It was a good thing it was dark, otherwise Calvin was sure to see I was blushing like an idiot. He was so sexy, everything he said and did turned me on to no end, but he'd been trying to get me to reciprocate with the dirty talk lately and I failed miserably at it. When a hot and horny mountain of a cop tells you to beg for his cock, you beg. But really, what exactly was he begging for when I tried?

"Sebastian?"

I shook my head. "What?"

"Something wrong?"

"No."

"You're getting soft."

God, this was embarrassing. "Nothing, really. I just… feel stupid trying to talk like you."

Calvin scooted up a bit, resting on his elbows. "Sebastian, you don't have to do anything you're not comfortable with."

"It's just talking, though," I said lamely.

"That doesn't matter. Do you want me to stop?"

"What? No. I love it when you do it," I said, feeling my entire face heat up. I took his hand and guided it back to my cock. "Sorry, I didn't mean to kill the mood."

"It's okay."

"Can we try again?"

In the faint gray light that came in through the bedroom window, Calvin appeared to be nodding before he lay back down. "Come here."

I leaned over him, the head of my cock bumping his lips. Calvin's tongue darted out, warm and wet, and I sighed and closed my eyes, rocking my hips gently.

"That's right," Calvin whispered. "Come here. Fuck my face." His hands came around to cup my ass again, pulling me toward him. He opened his mouth and took my cock, sucking eagerly.

"Shit," I swore quietly.

Reaching back to grab his hands, I yanked them up above his head and held them firmly. I rolled my hips again, a bit more enthusiastically when Calvin moaned in response. Watching him work my length with his throat was so goddamn hot.

I let go of one hand and wrapped mine around the back of his head, holding him in place. Even though I felt insecure as hell, I knew Calvin wanted me to talk. He got off on it, and sex was a two-way street. He couldn't do all the work and let me have all the fun.

So I manned up and told Calvin, "Take it all." I shoved in rougher, and he groaned loudly around my dick.

He reached down with his free hand to stroke himself quickly in time with my thrusts.

The wet, tight heat of Calvin's mouth after a week of not touching him was enough to send me over the edge like an inexperienced teenager. A prickle of sweat broke out across my body, and my stomach muscles tightened as I felt my orgasm coming.

"Oh God…. *Cal*." I let go of his other hand and gripped his hair in both hands, fucking his face hard and fast, like my very life depended on coming down his throat. "*Fuck*. I'm gonna—!"

I lost all capability to form thoughts at that point. It was too much. Calvin's mouth, his tongue, the heat between our bodies, but then a fingertip pressed gently into me, and I came with his name on my lips. My entire body shuddered as Calvin swallowed, and when I managed to pull free from his thoroughly fucked mouth, he tensed and came in his hand.

Moving down his body, I slid my arms under his, holding Calvin close as we both came down from that incredible high. "Jesus," I muttered. "I think I forgot my middle name."

His deep voice rumbled in his chest. "Speaking of, did you ever notice your initials spell SAS?"

"What are you trying to say?" I raised my head to look at him, brushing damp hair from Calvin's forehead.

"Aptly named. You're always a bit sassy," he teased.

"Uh-huh." I rolled off, taking a few deep breaths.

Calvin chuckled as he leaned over me, kissed my chest, and grabbed a tissue from the bedside table. He wiped himself clean before settling onto his side.

I rolled over and pressed up against his back, snaking an arm around his waist. I fell asleep like that. Blissful and content.

CHAPTER TWO

"You should have let me set the alarm last night."

"I can't believe I overslept."

"Your suit's in the closet."

"Max is calling you."

"Fuck." I grabbed my cell and walked out of the bedroom. "Are you at the shop already?"

"Already? It's nine. Where are you, boss?"

"I'm so sorry. I overslept," I said, wedging the phone against my ear and shoulder so I could crouch to tug my shoes on.

"Geez, that's a first."

"I know. I'm on my way. I'll be there soon."

"I'm going to go grab some coffee."

"No problem." I said good-bye, hung up, and stuffed my cell into my slacks. I bumped into Calvin in the bedroom doorway. "Want breakfast?" I asked, running in to fetch my sweater.

"No time," he called, knotting his tie and walking

into the living room. Calvin was already standing at the front door and buttoning his coat when I came back out of the bedroom.

I joined him, threw on my jacket and scarf, grabbed my shoulder bag, and barely had time to put my sunglasses on before following him out. I locked the door, and we raced down the rickety stairs to the ground floor. It was beginning to rain when we stepped outside. Not a lot, but enough to guarantee another cold, not entirely winter, but not quite spring day ahead.

Calvin surprised me when he took my face with one hand, tilted my head up, and kissed my mouth lightly. "Have a good day."

"You too."

He smiled and pulled his car keys from his pocket before hurrying down the sidewalk.

I dug my umbrella out of my bag and headed in the opposite direction. I was lucky to live so close to the Emporium that it was within easy walking distance, and I had no need for cabs or the subway. And thank God for that. With the way the MTA hiked up fares, who could justify the expense of a monthly pass these days? As for cabs, let's be honest, who actually thinks they'll get to work on time during morning rush hour by taking a taxi? Walking around folks who strolled, those attempting to text and walk, and early rising tourists was definitely the lesser of the evils.

On the Emporium's block was a man named Henry, who was standing under a large umbrella and doling out free newspapers to the passing crowds with the same chipper attitude and smile he'd had for the three years I'd been working here. I knew he was a native New Yorker because Henry was a talker and always had lots to tell me.

"Mr. Snow," Henry said with a big grin. "You're late!"

"Tell me about it." I accepted the folded newspaper he offered.

"No boyfriend today?" Henry had met Calvin exactly one time and had since asked me about him just about every day. I swear he was more smitten than I was.

"He's late for work as well," I clarified, already inching away.

Henry made a *tsk-tsk* sound and shook his head. "Don't work too hard."

"Yeah, you too," I said, waving the paper at him before hurrying toward the Emporium. I stopped at the shop, closed my umbrella, and froze in place before I had a chance to open the woven metal gate. Right there, on the sidewalk, was a brick. Just like the one thrown through my window yesterday.

"Hey, it's about time," Max called.

I turned around to see him rushing across the street with a take-out tray of coffee. He pulled his hood back as he reached me.

"Morning," I said distractedly.

"Morning to you. Must have been some night you had."

"What?" I glanced back up at Max.

He grinned lopsidedly. "Was there a certain redhead involved?"

I looked back down at the ground.

"Are you okay?"

I pointed at the brick. "Was this here when you first showed up?"

Max looked down. "Uh… I don't think so."

"No?"

"I don't remember seeing it."

I crouched, rain pattering on the cement. I picked

up the brick—it was dry underneath. "When did it start raining?" I squinted, looking up at Max.

"Maybe fifteen minutes ago."

"Not when you got here, though?"

"No," Max clarified. He shifted his weight from one foot to the other. "Are you sure nothing creepy is going on?"

"Positive," I lied as I stood, brick still in my hand. I offered it to Max, who held it like it was going to bite him, and I hurried to raise the gate.

So someone had left it there after Max called me and went for coffee, but before I'd hardly gotten out of my apartment when the rain started....

I unlocked the front door and pushed it—only for it to resist opening. I could hear the beeping of the security system and swore. I only had a few seconds to turn it off before it began wailing. I gave the door another serious shove and heard the strange sound of *bricks* clatter together. After managing enough space to squeeze into the shop, I nearly tripped when the floor was higher than it was yesterday.

That was mighty strange.

I grabbed the wall, leaned in close to the security system, punched in the code, and waited for the light to flash a gray shade I'd been told was green before letting out a breath.

"What the hell is going on?" Max asked.

"I don't know." I wiggled back out of the small opening, then shoved the door hard. More loud scraping and scratching across my antique wood floor. I reached in and switched on the rarely used overhead lights, wincing and looking away.

Max muttered, "This is so messed up."

I cracked open one eye and looked back into the

shop. Still wearing my sunglasses helped me see the bricks that were *everywhere*. "The hell…?" I whispered.

Max slowly crouched and set the brick in his hand back on the ground. He stood again, and I could hear him swallow. He laughed nervously. "If only they were yellow."

"Huh?"

"Follow the yellow brick road."

"Where does the gray road lead?" I asked before taking a step inside.

"Seb, wait. Maybe we should call the cops."

The bricks shifted under my feet as I walked across the floor. I paused in front of the first display and glanced around to either side. The bricks kept going toward the far end of the shop, where the maps and back door was. I took the right aisle, moving to the counter. Sure enough, there were bricks on the steps and on the elevated floor.

"Seb?" Max called, still standing at the open door.

"Yeah? Hold on." I tiptoed around bricks as I went to the counter.

One brick sat beside the brass register, a rubber band around it. Carefully, I picked it up, turned it around, and tugged free a slip of paper from its corner. I unfolded it, heart racing as I did. It looked like regular, lined notebook paper. Nothing fancy and nothing unique. And written in the middle was one word.

Curious?

"Curiouser and curiouser," I whispered in agreement.

"You're such a Luddite, Seb," Max said as he leaned over me at the computer in my office.

"Calvin had this all set up for me. I never thought I'd seriously have to go through security footage to capture the mad bricklayer."

After it had been learned in December that Duncan Andrews had somehow swiped my keys and made copies to sneak in and out of the Emporium and my apartment, Calvin had been… *firm* that my security cameras be fixed and upgraded. They recorded and dumped footage wirelessly, and I could go through it all at my leisure. There were two angles: one was on the register from behind, to have a view of both the customers and who was handling money; the other on the front door at an angle to include some of the more expensive displays.

Max had the footage on fast-forward throughout the night, both of us watching the screen intently and waiting for the intruder to appear. At just after four in the morning, one of the cameras went black. Then the second.

"Whoa, wait," I said, waving a hand. "What happened?"

"I don't know." Max paused and went back. "It's hard to—what is that—are they painted over?"

I stood from the computer desk and went to the register, stumbling over bricks. I grabbed a stepladder from the nearby corner, and after making some space on the floor, climbed up to examine the camera. I reached out to touch the lens, then scraped gently at it with my nail.

"So?" Max called from the doorway.

I held my finger close, squinting at the little flakes that came away. "Spray paint maybe?"

"Are you shitting me? That's so Hollywood."

I wiped my hand on my sweater and climbed down. "No one came in the front, so they must have broken through the back door." I put my hands on my hips, frowning. "But why wasn't the alarm tripped?"

Max shrugged. "How long do they have to turn it off before it notifies the company?"

"Not long enough to climb ladders and spray-paint the cameras." I looked back at Max and pulled my phone free. "Just after four, right?"

He nodded.

I gave my security company a call, but the man on the other line insisted that nothing had triggered the alarm.

"I have footage of someone in the shop. Well, I have footage of the cameras being blacked out. By *someone*."

"I understand, Mr. Snow," the man replied. "But your system looks to be working fine. There are no malfunctions, and there were no indications of someone entering the store last night. My date stamp from yesterday is the alarm being activated at 6:23—"

"Yes, that was me leaving."

"And this morning it was disabled at 9:19."

"Me again."

The man was quiet for a beat, and I could hear the muted sound of keys typing away. "I have nothing else recorded."

"If no one broke in… I mean, someone had to have disabled the alarm."

"There's nothing, sir."

"Then my system isn't working like you think it is," I said, starting to get rightfully pissed. "Someone was in here at four in the morning. My cameras were blacked out and the entire shop is full of bricks!"

"Full of what?"

"Not the point!" I shouted.

"I understand you're upset, Mr. Snow. If you can wait on the line, I'm going to—"

"Forget it. I need to call the cops and have something actually done." I hung up, cussing loudly.

"Wow," Max said, still standing in the office

doorway. "I've never seen you get angry like that."

"Advice Line says nothing happened," I snapped. "How can they say that? Look at this place. If someone had the time to do this, and the motion sensors never went off, what the hell kind of service am I paying for?"

Max nodded obediently.

So I called the cops.

Again.

And it turned out to be the same officers from yesterday. Their coats and hats were wet when they entered the shop, both hesitating at stepping into the sea of bricks.

"Good morning, officers," I said, making my way toward them.

The woman took her hat off. "Mr. Snow. Should we put your shop on our list of routine check-ins?"

God, I hoped she was joking.

"Ha…." I cleared my throat and squinted in the harsh lighting to read her badge.

Bridge? No, Brigg.

That's right. I recalled her name now from Christmas.

"What seems to be… happening here?" Brigg asked.

"I wish I knew," I answered, motioning vaguely at the area around us. "When I got here this morning, there was a brick outside the front door. And as you can see, the shop was full of them when I opened up. But the doors were locked, the alarms never went off, and the gate was down."

She put her hands on her belt. "I see."

"I have footage of my cameras getting blacked out just after four this morning. Someone, I think from out of the frame, spray-painted the lenses. They must have come in through the back, but my alarm company is insistent that they never received any indication of trouble."

The officers looked at each other.

"And I'm inclined to believe it wasn't a ghost," I added dryly.

"Do you have anything to report as missing?" Brigg asked.

"No, nothing," I said, shaking my head.

"Can you show us the back door?" Lowry asked.

"Sure." I turned and carefully made my way through the aisles toward the back of the building. I unlocked the door and pushed it open to reveal the chilly but mostly dry alley I shared with Beth Harrison of Good Books.

I stepped out first, shivering. The alley was odd and connected our shops together, but it wasn't insulated from the weather by any means. I looked up and down, hoping to find some obvious evidence as to who was trying to remodel my shop. Like footprints, or wheelbarrow tracks, or a signed and notarized letter from the guilty party.

"Well," Brigg started, examining the door's lock. "Not broken, no sign of forced entry. Is your landlord doing any sort of work on the building?"

I resisted the urge to be a smartass, and before coffee, it hurt like hell to keep the knee-jerk response to myself. "Uh, even if he was, don't you think someone would have triggered the alarm?"

She nodded absently, pondering the information available. "You've got a mystery on your hands, Mr. Snow."

"Looks like."

"We'll file another report," she continued. "Someone clearly has trespassed, but with no security footage and the fact that nothing was taken, there isn't much for us to investigate, you understand."

I nodded and stuffed my hands into my pockets. I could have told them about the second note then. I should have told them. I *should* have given it to them to analyze. But I didn't.

This was personal.

Curious?

Damn right I was.

"I suggest having all of the locks changed," Brigg said. "New keys, new code for the alarm—maybe have a technician come out and make sure it's not malfunctioning."

"Yes, ma'am," I answered automatically.

I followed the officers back into the store, shutting and locking the door to the alley. I thanked them for their time, agreed to call if anything new came to light, and then saw them out. At the front door, I flicked off the overhead lights.

"Hey!" Max called from the darkness. "I can't see shit."

"You're fine. Turn on the lamps," I said back, watching the police get into their cruiser and pull away from the curb.

Behind me, I heard the snap of an old bank lamp turning on, followed by the shifting sound of bricks under Max's feet as he walked around the shop. "So what now?" Max asked.

"I'm going next door."

"Why?"

"To check in with Beth."

"She does seem a likely suspect," Max said in a thoughtful tone.

I snorted at the image of plump little Beth, with her big glasses and gray hair and wearing clothing with cats on them, busily covering the Emporium floor space in bricks. Yeah, she was at the top of my persons-of-interest list. I rolled my eyes, pushed up my sunglasses, and walked out the door.

I ducked under her awning and opened the door to the bookshop. It was much more brightly lit than my store, although crammed with enough second-hand books to make me feel right at home amongst the organized chaos. The radio overhead was playing sappy, poppy love songs in lieu of Valentine's Day this coming Sunday.

Shit. Was it really this Sunday?

Standing on the welcome mat in Good Books wasn't the best place for it to occur to me that I wasn't entirely certain if Calvin and I would celebrate Valentine's Day. I mean, sure we were dating, and it was a lovey-dovey, couples-centric holiday, but did Calvin like that sort of stuff?

Did *I*, for that matter?

Sort of.

Not that I'd admit it to anyone.

"What are you doing here so early, Sebby?"

I pushed the poorly timed thoughts out of mind and turned to the counter. Beth stood at the register with an expectant look, eyeing me through her thick glasses. What did we have today? I squinted. A sweater with a big cat face. The eyes were made of buttons and the cat had a bow on its head. It was actually kind of terrifying.

"Beth." I looked around, spotting a few customers already perusing her aisles. I walked to the counter and leaned over. "Has anything strange happened over here in the past day or so?"

She quirked a brow. "Strange? I've sold all of my tofu cookbooks. I've been wondering if there's a new health fad happening. Is there? With tofu?"

"What? No. I mean, I've no idea. Listen. Yesterday someone smashed one of my windows."

"*Son of a bitch*," she shouted. "I was wondering what was up with the plywood when I walked by this morning."

"Yeah. Anyway, this morning when I opened the Emporium, the entire shop was full of bricks."

"Come again?"

"Bricks," I repeated.

"Like, for building?" Beth asked, confused.

"Yes."

"Why?"

"I wish I could tell you." I leaned a bit closer. "Someone broke in. They must have disabled my security system somehow. I wanted to make sure nothing odd has happened here."

Beth scoffed and waved a hand. "Here? Come on, I don't piss folks off."

"No? You might. You curse like a drunken sailor, Beth."

"*You're* the one who dated a crazy person."

"I did not date him," I clarified while holding a finger up. "Duncan *thought* he was dating me. Big difference."

Beth shrugged. "No one's put bricks in here. Sorry, Sebby. Do you need help cleaning?"

"There's too many."

"I'm not some old granny who can't pick up a few bricks!"

I pulled my cell out, opened up a photo I had taken before the police arrived, and turned the screen around to show her.

Beth snorted. "Better hire a moving company."

"Or construction. How much do you think I can sell these for?" I asked, putting my phone away.

"I'd say you'd make enough to buy you and your hunky guy a nice dinner."

Luther returned for the second time in two days, which was twice as many times as I wanted to see my landlord. He patted his big belly while eyeing the shop, took a step forward, but when the bricks wiggled under his unsteady footing, he stopped. "What did you do? I said I was fixing the window."

"I didn't do this," I exclaimed.

Trying to explain the situation to him was like debating with a—well, a brick wall. I hated my landlord for many reasons. But mostly because he's an idiot.

"The police advised me to get new locks," I said. "I know they didn't come through the front door, so the gate is fine. It's the alley. I need better security on the back door."

"How do you even know that if the cameras were blacked out?"

I heard Max make a noise behind me from the counter, and I rubbed my unshaven chin in agitation. "Someone took out the cameras from the inside, without being seen, Mr. North. If they came through the back, moved along the walls, and approached the camera from behind—"

As I explained to him how it must have happened, it was like an explosion of fireworks going off in my head.

In order to do that, to know where the cameras couldn't pick someone up, they would have to be familiar with the layout of the Emporium. So this dude with the brick fetish must have come in before as a customer. Just like with Duncan Andrews.

Had I mistakenly placed a newspaper ad that encouraged psychopaths to visit my shop?

Luther humphed loudly. "And?"

"I, uh—so I need new locks."

"I guess I can see about getting some installed over

the weekend."

"I'm open on the weekend. I'm only closed on Monday, and I'm not waiting until next week. If this isn't dealt with today, who knows what could happen. Do I need to remind you how much my Victrola is worth?" I turned to point at the large furniture on one side of the room.

Luther waved a meaty hand at me, speaking over the shop phone ringing. "Fine, fine, fine. I'll have my guys come by during lunch. They'll deal with the locks and the window."

"And the bricks?"

"Put them in the alley and I'll see that they're removed."

"By myself?" I retorted.

"Seb?" Max called.

"Not now," I answered. "There's like two hundred bricks in here."

"I'm not paying my guys to—"

"I'm not going to break my back picking them all up," I said over Luther.

"Seb," Max called again.

"*What*?" I asked, aggravated, as I turned around.

He waved the phone. "It's Quinn Lancaster."

My heart stopped. I felt a weird sort of fear wash over my body, where I was hot and cold at the same time, breathing fast but not getting air to my lungs. Why would Calvin's partner call me for any reason other than something happened to him? With the current rift between him and his family, I was all Calvin had.

Did that make me his emergency contact?

I swallowed the sour taste threatening to come up my throat, quickly scrambled across the uneven floor to the counter, and grabbed the phone from Max. "Hello? Quinn?"

"Hi, Sebastian."

"Is he okay?"

"What?"

"Calvin."

"Sure he is. Why are you asking?"

I rested my elbows on the counter and pressed a hand to my forehead. "I didn't think—why are you calling?"

After a beat, I heard Quinn sigh. "Oh, sorry. I didn't mean to make you think this was official. But that's sweet, your response."

"It's not sweet. I nearly barfed."

"Calvin and I are getting a late breakfast. I thought it'd be nice if you joined us."

"Really?" I'd never been invited to see Calvin during work hours. He was simply too busy. And he didn't usually eat while working. Something was wrong. "Isn't he sort of swamped?"

"No."

"I—oh." I glanced back over my shoulder. Luther was busying himself by looking through a display of trinkets. "Slow day for murders, huh?"

"It's been fairly calm lately."

Since when? "I guess I assumed it was a heavy workload lately. I don't see him that much," I said quietly.

She hummed in response. I got the distinct impression that Calvin or someone else she didn't want hearing was close enough to listen to her call. "That's why I thought it'd be nice to take a break. Cold cases can wait an hour."

I'm not sure what I was feeling at that moment. Confusion, for sure. I always suspected Calvin was swamped with big cases, based on how often I saw him, but was this not true? Was he working late into the night, not sleeping and eating right, because he was working on cold cases? I didn't want to believe I was always his top priority—it seemed selfish because I knew how deeply he cared about his job—but still.

Shouldn't he have wanted to come home to me if he had the option? And what was Quinn trying to tell me? Was she concerned about his overworking? Not that I wasn't, but she saw more of him than I did. Maybe she could see warning signs he hid from me. Calvin buried himself in work because when he was focused on a task, atrocities he saw during the war could be put out of mind.

But what if they were starting to affect him during the day? Not just when he slept.

Suddenly nothing else was important.

"Where am I meeting you?"

CHAPTER THREE

Saul's Diner's slogan was "Get stuffed."

But brunch was neither the time nor the place for that.

Saul's was an old place, midway between my shop and Calvin's precinct. The food was good—not great, but good. And cheap. And it was open 24/7.

I had reached the diner before Quinn and Calvin and chose a booth near the back, opposite of the windows lining the street-side wall. A waitress poured me a cup of coffee and let me be when I told her I was waiting for company.

Pouring some cream into the mug, I stirred it before letting out a sigh and turned to stare out the windows. The rain was coming down hard now, the gray day easy on my eyes. There was something about heavy rain in an urban environment that I had always found kind of depressing. Not that I left the city all that often to compare it to rain in the country or suburbs, but it gave off a sort of isolated feeling.

Everyone was in a rush to get out of the weather. No one mingled, chatted—it made it lonely. *I* wasn't lonely, though. I definitely wasn't. Not anymore. But I *was* worried, and the general gloom of the day was fraying my nerves.

The worry had been directed toward my business and livelihood first. Vandalism and trespassing. Would it escalate? Would someone get hurt? Specifically, me. Those notes weren't just anything. They were *something*.

But then Quinn calling?

Calvin hadn't appeared to be getting worse to me. He still had nightmares, of course. He hadn't magically gotten better by dating me. I'd been with him through a few more since Christmas, and to see him at his most vulnerable and exposed moments hurt my heart like nothing else. It was worse to think Quinn had noticed something to be concerned about and I hadn't. Or that Calvin still didn't trust me enough to talk about it.

Maybe trust isn't the right word.

I put my head down on the table.

I think Calvin was afraid to talk about what he had seen overseas. Words gave power, after all, and I guess he figured the memories would truly consume him if he gave them acknowledgment. I only wished there was a way to help him understand that he could find strength for *himself* in speaking about those events. But it wasn't something I was comfortable pressing him with. Every time I even hesitantly approached the subject, he went on the defense.

"Howdy, partner."

I raised my head to see Quinn standing at the booth, hands in her coat pockets, and grinning. "Morning."

She slid into the seat across from me. "Thanks for coming. I haven't seen you in a while."

"Oh, sure. Thanks. How've you been?"

"Good." Quinn picked up her napkin and wiped her hands on it absently. "Except that I haven't had a smoke all morning and Calvin won't let me in his car with a cigarillo."

"Maybe you aren't asking nicely."

"They're vanilla," she protested, crumpling the napkin and setting it aside.

"Calvin's more of a cinnamon guy."

She made a face and picked up the plastic menu from the tabletop. "Speaking of," I started. "Where is he?"

"Hey, sweetie."

I startled and looked up again. Calvin was shaking off his wet coat as he approached the table. I smiled. He gave me butterflies whenever he addressed me by a pet name in public. "Hi."

He slid into the booth beside me. "Didn't expect to see you here."

"I didn't expect to be here."

He nodded, reaching to unbutton his cuffs and roll his sleeves back. "Is Max watching the Emporium?"

"Yeah. I have to bring him back food or he may quit."

The waitress returned with coffee for Calvin and Quinn before taking our orders.

Quinn grabbed a handful of sugar packets and poured them into her mug as we were left alone again. "So how's your little shop?"

"It's fine," I said politely.

Calvin leaned back, placing his arm across the top of the seat to rest behind me. It was like the teenage boy sitting on a couch beside his crush, so he acts like he's stretching to put an arm around them. Except that Calvin was way more cool about it.

Quinn nodded as she finished drowning her coffee in sugar. "Calvin told me this morning someone busted a window?"

"That's right. I—oh." I hesitated. I had declined to tell Officer Brigg and Officer Lowry about the second note, but to not tell Calvin seemed stupid. Keeping something like that from him would undoubtedly cause a domestic dispute if he found out through work.

And besides, I was retired from sleuthing.

No matter how curious I was about these notes.

I reached into my sweater and pulled out the second slip of paper. "I got another note today."

"You what?" Calvin asked, setting his mug down and turning his attention to me.

"Note?" Quinn piped up.

I handed it to Calvin. "It was wrapped around a brick on the counter." When he glanced up from the message, I explained everything, from the brick outside to the police to Luther's second visit.

Hearing myself say it all out loud, I sounded insane.

Someone breaking into my store?

Harassing me with bricks and nonthreatening messages?

No wonder Quinn was giving me a peculiar expression as I finished. "Well," she began. "That's fucking weird."

I leaned sideways to stare at the one word on the letter that Calvin still held.

Curious?

Yes. And now, so were others.

The bricks were intentionally chosen. They had to be. They were so unexpected, so odd, that it got people talking. And when you want folks invested in their own curiosity, you have to nourish it.

"Barnum," I stated, sort of surprised at the thought.

Calvin looked at me while folding the letter. "Hmm?"

"P.T. Barnum," I said again. "That's what this whole thing reminds me of."

"The circus guy?" Quinn asked.

I nodded, took the letter from Calvin, and stuffed it in my pocket. "But before he went into the circus business, he used to own a museum here in New York. He hired some guy to walk around the block with bricks, putting one on each corner before going into the museum, walking through it, and slipping out the back to go through the process again. The brick thing was so strange that people started getting curious and following him. They'd pay to enter the museum but would then be sidetracked by the displays."

Quinn snorted. "Correction. *That's* fucking weird."

I shrugged. "Barnum was a brilliant businessman. He knew in order for people to give a crap about his curiosities, he needed them to be… curious." I looked at Calvin, and he was staring hard at me with an unreadable, very cop-like, expression.

"Why do you know this?" Quinn asked.

I glanced at her. "I know a lot about nothing of real importance."

"That's not true," Calvin said. "You're brilliant and it gets you in trouble."

I put my hands up in surrender. "I didn't do anything."

"Yet," Calvin replied in a deep tone.

"Oh, come on, Cal. I was only relating one stupid thing to another. I don't think Barnum is haunting my shop—I'm not about to try my skills at ghost hunting."

"I didn't say anything of the sort," Calvin answered. "It's not a dead person fucking with you, baby. It's someone very much alive, and I want you to be careful. Anything else happens, you call me right away."

The waitress returned and put down plates heaped with food.

Get stuffed, all right.

An acceptable silence fell over us as we ate.

I pushed the thoughts of the notes to the back of my mind. Letting myself ruminate over them was only going to lead to trouble. And I wasn't going to get involved.

No sleuthing.

No sleuthing.

No sleuthing.

Calvin reached under the tabletop, set his hand on my thigh, and gave it a light squeeze. "You okay?" he murmured around bites of pancakes.

I nodded quickly, looking up. "Yup. Fine."

"You're not eating."

"Sorry. I'm shitty at multitasking. I can't eat and think." I picked up my fork and dug into the now semicold omelet.

"What're you—"

He was interrupted by a loud crash from the kitchen. His hand on my thigh tightened painfully as he jumped in his seat.

"Calvin?" I immediately put a hand on his shoulder.

He jumped again at my touch and let out a panicked, held breath. Calvin looked between me and Quinn before quickly getting up from the booth. "Excuse me," he whispered.

"Calvin? Wait!" I watched him make for the restrooms.

"Go check on him," Quinn said quickly. "Please."

I nodded, already getting to my feet and running after

him before he had a chance to lock the door behind him. "Cal," I said, pushing the door open against his forceful hold. "Let me in."

"I'm fine," he said, sounding ragged.

"No, let me in," I ordered, shoving hard and squirming in through the opening before letting the door slam shut.

The lighting was harsh and made me wince. Calvin was a little blurry, a little too bright, and appeared to be almost in tears. He backed up against the opposite wall, covering his face and taking deep breaths. His shoulders slumped. That was my cue.

I moved forward and pulled him against me as he started sobbing. Calvin wrapped his arms tight around me, burying his face against my neck and shoulder. Calvin was a big man. If it wasn't for his recent shoulder injury, he could easily lift me. So when he put all of his muscle weight against me, it was difficult to keep us both standing.

His grip on me was so hard, it nearly hurt.

"It's okay," I whispered, petting his hair. "It's okay." I never knew what else to tell him when he was having an episode.

"I'm so sorry," Calvin cried.

"No, don't be sorry," I insisted.

I couldn't hold us both up anymore, so I awkwardly maneuvered Calvin back against the wall and eased him to the floor. He pulled his legs up, and I sat on my knees between them. I leaned over to grab a paper towel from the dispenser, then pulled his hand from his face and wiped his cheeks dry. The muscles in Calvin's neck tightened as he clenched his jaw.

Calvin let out another breath after a moment, a gasp like he was drowning. He tilted his head back to stare at the ceiling. "He was a nineteen-year-old kid on his first tour, and I watched him get blown to pieces."

I didn't move. I hesitated even to breathe. This was the first time Calvin had really said anything about his terrors, the memories he relived over and over that seemed to be haunting him in his waking hours now.

His fragile composure broke again, and Calvin began to cry once more. He didn't say anything else about what the dropped plates had reminded him of. I didn't want to know about the boy Calvin had seen die, but if it meant taking that pain away from him, I'd soak in every god-awful detail.

Once Calvin began to calm down, I wiped his face dry again.

He reached both hands out, put them on my waist, and tugged me close enough to kiss. "I didn't mean for that to happen," he whispered.

I combed my fingers through his thick hair. "Cal. Is there anything we can talk about?"

Calvin didn't reply, looking sort of lost.

"I mean—and please, I'm not trying to upset you, I swear—I think Quinn is concerned about you."

That made him frown.

"You have a stressful job. We don't want you to get hurt, is all."

"It has nothing to do with my job," Calvin said sternly.

"No. I know that. But… maybe it's wearing you out mentally and making you more susceptible to these moments."

"It's not," he said with a tone of finality.

I sighed and looked down at the paper towel in my hand. It always ended this way. Always. No matter what I said. "Calvin, this scares me," I whispered.

"I'm fine."

"You're *not* fine," I said quickly. "You just had an epic meltdown in a diner bathroom. All I'm asking is to consider going to a VA—"

"Stop it." Calvin maneuvered me back so he could stand.

"Calvin," I said, getting up after him.

He ignored me, opened the bathroom door, and walked out.

I threw my hands up, watching the door close. This was like beating a dead horse. I didn't know how else to get through to him. I couldn't force Calvin to seek help, but he wasn't even willing to look at how much this concerned me.

I'm fine.

Like hell.

I tossed the paper towel and walked out. I turned right, walking back to the booths in time to see Calvin buttoning his coat and Quinn standing, following suit. "Where are you going?" I asked gently.

"Back to work," he said, not looking at me.

"But—Calvin—"

He pulled his wallet from his back pocket and put a few bills down on the table. "This should cover breakfast."

"Wait—"

Calvin was already walking away, and my stomach dropped as if I were on the worst roller-coaster ride of my life.

Quinn looked at me.

I shook my head. "I don't know."

She frowned while fixing the collar of her coat. "I'll make sure he goes home tonight."

I nodded, feeling numb. "You can call me… if you need to."

"I will." She turned and left after Calvin.

I stayed behind to pay for the half-eaten meals.

There are a surprising number of brick sellers in the New York metro area.

Sitting at the computer in my office, I squinted and leaned in. I had come back to the Emporium less than psyched with life and fell into one of my known nasty habits. When something is out of my control, I obsess about what *is* in my control. So if I couldn't help Calvin and he didn't want to talk to me, by God I was going to figure out who the fuck was harassing my shop. But this wasn't sleuthing. I was just researching.

I had thought maybe I could call a few companies and ask if they'd sold a large quantity of bricks in the last few days, since it would be hard to conceal a few hundred of them in New York City for an extended period of time. But not only did big chain stores like Home Depot sell bricks, there were a number of small mom-and-pop shops within the five boroughs that did as well.

And the bricks weren't exactly unique. If they had been bedazzled with sequins, this search would be a hell of a lot easier.

I still tried calling a few places. Logically I stayed away from locations in Jersey, as they seemed the most unlikely. Home Depot said there was no way they could share sales information and hung up on me. A shop in the Bronx didn't understand what I was asking, and after the old guy said, "Eh? Eh? What do you mean?" three times, *I* disconnected.

Third on my list was a Brooklyn store, Mortar and More. I dialed the number on my cell and put it to my ear.

"Mortar and More. This is Louise. How can I help

you?"

"Hi," I said, sitting up. "I have sort of a strange request and was hoping to talk to someone in sales?"

"You can talk to me, honey. What do you need?"

"I'm wondering if you can tell me about anyone who may have bought about two hundred bricks from you within the past few days."

She was quiet for a moment. "Why's that?"

"Someone's pulled a prank on my business, and honestly I'm just trying to find out who, since the police are sort of at a loss."

"Unfortunately I can't give out the names of our customers, dear."

I pinched the bridge of my nose. "Are you able to just say whether you've sold that number recently?"

"We sell thousands of bricks," Louise answered. "Every week."

"But I'm specifically looking for—"

"Sorry," she said. "You understand, as a business owner yourself, I can't just give out people's names and contact information. Good luck." She hung up.

I growled and put my cell down. This was a pointless effort. It was a good try, but this was going to be my response everywhere. Hell, if someone called me like this, I'd tell them to fuck off too.

"Seb?"

I turned to the door.

Max jutted his thumb behind him. "It's getting kind of busy with customers and those construction dudes. Can you help me finish cleaning?"

"Sorry. Yeah, I'm done." I stood and followed him to the front of the Emporium.

Luther's workers were in the middle of installing

my new window and making plenty of noise. Naturally I also had several customers on the floor at that time. And the fucking bricks were still in here. Granted, while I was out, the workers had helped Max move them to the back door, but they left the massive pile there, and my floor was covered in dust.

Max assisted customers at checkout while I grabbed a broom and made quick work of the mess, sweeping it all toward the back. I opened the door and swept the dust into the alley. *You're welcome, Luther.* Setting the broom aside after, I started picking up the bricks one by one and piling them into the alley for my landlord to haul away.

It was only after I'd been at this for several moments that I took notice of the bricks in my hands as being different shades. The world existed to me in varying types of gray, due to my achromatopsia, but in reduced lighting, I could still clearly tell when colors differed. To an extent I could even guess colors, but only when it was sort of obvious, like grass was green, my hair was brown, the ocean was blue. These all have unique shades when seen as gray.

My world is vibrant, in its own sense.

So when I turned and went back to the pile of bricks and really started to look, there were a number of mismatching shades. And that told me that there was no way these were bought in a large number from a modern shop. I shut the back door with my foot and crouched down to start examining the bricks.

Some were even and well made; others had small chips or weren't quite uniform, as if they hadn't stood the test of time. Most felt well-worn in my hands—so definitely not new. I started pawing through the pile more quickly, finding an abundance that had stampings on them, but it was hard to read. I pulled my magnifying glass from my sweater pocket and held it up to the brick.

Boff—no—Buffalo Blocks.

Huh.

"What're you doing?"

I looked over my shoulder to see Max staring down at me. "Hey." I motioned toward the pile. "These aren't the same colors, are they?"

"Uh, I guess not."

"What color?"

"Brick color."

"You're fucking hysterical," I said.

Max shrugged. "What's it matter? They're like a reddish color. Some are a bit darker, a not really purple. It's hard to say."

"But definitely not matching," I concluded.

"No," Max said, shaking his head. "Does that mean something?"

I turned to stare at the pile again. "I don't know. Maybe. They're old."

"Want to sell them?" Max asked, and I wasn't sure if he was joking.

"What I mean is, they weren't purchased from a store around here, you know? And this…," I said, raising the brick I had been reading. "Buffalo Blocks."

"Should that mean something to me? Hey. Is this like one huge, elaborate test to see if I know as much random shit as you? Am I up for a raise?"

"No, it's not a test, and no, you get no raise, since you failed."

"You said it wasn't a test."

I shrugged and looked at the brick once more. "Oh. I think this is Buffalo, Kansas."

Max grumbled.

I set the brick down and wiped my hands on my

slacks while standing.

"Wait a minute," Max said, breaking my concentration. "I know that look."

I turned to him, raising a brow. "Come again?"

"The weird crease you get here when you're thinking too hard," he said, touching his own forehead. "You're not sleuthing, are you?"

"No." I moved by before Max could say another word, and went to help a customer.

I was drained by the time I made it to my apartment building that evening. Calvin hadn't called me, I was worried about him after his meltdown at Saul's, and I hadn't had any time to research the antique bricks because I was supposed to be running a business. I dragged my ass up the three flights of stairs and caught my neighbor unlocking her door across from mine.

She turned and smiled shyly. "Hi, Mr. Snow."

I knew her name was Sally Ng, because it was on her mailbox downstairs. Likewise, she probably only knew my last name, because that was all I had put on my tag. "Good evening," I said.

"Hey—uhm—is your boyfriend a cop?" she asked, lingering in her doorway.

I paused, keys in hand, looking at her again. "Yeah. Why?"

Sally shrugged. She was so tiny, it felt as if I were talking to a kid with the way I had to look down at her. "I saw his gun once."

"Oh. Right. He's a detective. Don't worry."

She smiled. "That's good."

"I hope you weren't scared."

"No. He's nice."

I nodded. That he was. "Well. Have a good night."

Sally stepped into her apartment. "You too." She shut the door.

Ah.

Awkward small talk between people living practically on top of each other. I was pondering how old Sally was, since we had been neighbors for several years now, as I shoved open my front door.

But then I saw the body on the floor.

CHAPTER FOUR

I didn't move.

Didn't speak.

The only sound that seemed to penetrate the bubble around me was the quiet clatter of plates from Sally's apartment and the clanking of the pipes as the building's heat turned on for the evening.

The body in the middle of my living room floor seemed quite undisturbed.

I swallowed the lump lodged in my throat and took a hesitant step inside. I quietly shut the door behind me, as if the maybe-dead guy would give a shit whether I slammed it or not. My bag slid off my shoulder and hit the floor with a thud.

No movement.

Not even a twitch.

But what if he were alive? Was this a trap? Who was it?

I glanced to either side of me for a weapon. For

nearly three weeks, I had had an antique fireplace kit beside the front door that I had neglected to drag to the Emporium because it was heavy. Now I really wished I hadn't gotten Calvin to drive it in for me, because being able to whack this son of a bitch upside the skull with a poker seemed like the best idea at the moment. Instead, I grabbed a big dictionary that sat on the small table I usually tossed my keys on.

So great. If this asshole tried anything funny, I could teach him the meaning of trespassing. Quite literally.

"All right," I said, finding my voice. "I'm coming over there, and don't you dare move," I ordered. "If you so much as twitch, I'll smack you so hard, your unborn children will know the meaning of words like *bardolatry*."

I gripped the dictionary tight and slowly crept forward. The room was only illuminated by city lights that bled in through the windows by the table, and the dimness allowed me to make out peculiar clothing the—I think—man was wearing.

What the hell?

A petticoat?

I stopped beside the body and reluctantly nudged the boot with my own foot.

No response.

I crouched down, setting the dictionary aside. The man lay on his stomach, face turned away from me. I should have gotten up, should have run out the door and called the police. But I'm the cat that curiosity keeps trying to kill. I pulled the sleeves of my coat over my hands and heaved the guy onto his back.

There was a dark spot on my floor that matched his chest, and my stomach rolled. I didn't need to get closer—I could smell the blood. The guy's eyes were open, and he had a dead, vacant expression. His hair was oddly styled, and he had a weird little beard. For some reason that stuck with me. He looked like a man who reenacted the Civil War. That was the first thought I had, minus the fact that he was wearing old-style women's clothing.

As if this couldn't get any fucking more bizarre, I noticed a slip of paper sticking up from his coat pocket. My hands shook as I leaned over and tugged it free by the corner. I unfolded the regular notebook paper with some blood on it.

It began with a fire.

I dropped the letter, my hands shaking too much by then. Nope, I was done with this. I stood, taking several steps back while fighting to free my cell from my pocket. I called Calvin.

He answered, thank God.

"Hey," he said, sounding tired.

"T-there's a dead guy in my apartment!" I shouted into the phone.

A beat. "*What?*"

"Holy shit, Cal. What do I do?"

"Get out," Calvin said immediately. "Get out of the building, right now. Go somewhere safe. I'm on my way."

"Okay," I said automatically, already moving to the door. "I'll go across the street to the coffee shop."

"Wait there. Don't move from that spot, understand? Ten minutes, I promise."

I hung up and slid my phone into my pocket again. Without a second thought, I grabbed my keys and ran out.

I locked the door—I'm not sure why—and was halfway down the stairs when the building shook and burst into flames.

My head hurt and it was hard to breathe. I was lying in the stairwell, drywall and broken banisters littering me and the floor. I could hear fire alarms going off above and below me. Blood was dripping down my neck.

I couldn't see.

Where were my sunglasses?

The building shook violently once more, and it protested and groaned loudly, more debris falling from above. I curled into a ball, covering my head as parts of the ceiling landed on me. I peeked up after a moment. Everything was extremely blurry—foggy even.

Smoke.

I smelled burning.

Someone was screaming.

I struggled to my feet, coughing and feeling lightheaded. Instinct told me to run. I was a flight and a half from the front door, and that's where safety was. That's where Calvin would be. But someone was still screaming and crying.

Then I realized it was my neighbor.

"Sally?" I called out, voice drowned by the creaking and splintering of wood. "Sally!" I tried again. I raced back up the stairs.

Or what was left of them.

I tripped and stumbled my way back to the third floor, but it wasn't there anymore.

I couldn't reach the landing because it was full of debris. Through bits of it, I could feel wisps of cold air.

My apartment was *gone*.

"Help!" Sally screamed again, her calls briefly followed by terrified crying.

"Sally, it's Sebastian. Where are you?" I shouted over the noise of everything breaking and falling apart.

I followed her pleas for help to a wedge of space where a support beam had fallen, which seemed to be all that was now keeping the wall from collapsing in on the stairwell. I crouched down and started shoving and pulling debris out of the way, tossing it aside before grabbing her outstretched hand.

"I've got you," I said firmly.

I was shit scared.

I'd never experienced a rush of adrenaline like this in my entire life.

But I couldn't just let her die there.

"Sally, come on," I called out to her. "You've got to help me get this crap out of the way!"

And maybe it was because she knew someone was there to get her out, but Sally stopped crying. From what I could see of her arms, she was determinedly pushing wreckage my way to make a small opening.

I leaned in close, making out what I could of her. "Are you okay?"

"Yes! Please don't leave me."

"I won't, I promise. Give me your hands. I'll pull."

She stuck her arms out of the space, and I grabbed and yanked for all it was worth.

Thank God she was tiny.

Sally slid free. She was bleeding and coughing up a lung, but her arms and legs were moving and she generally seemed to be in one piece. She immediately started crying again and grabbed me.

Above us was another explosion, and the building shook. We both screamed, and I pulled her close, covering her with my body as shit fell on us.

"Sally, hey, it's going to be okay," I insisted, because if I didn't, who would? "But I lost my glasses and I can't see, so I need your help."

That seemed to give her a strange source of courage. "Okay," she said. Sally grabbed my hand tight.

We both started down the stairs, and they were breaking behind us as we moved. The old building was going to fall in on itself any second. I grabbed at the hot wall to guide me, and Sally pushed me in the right direction as I led the way. We reached the first floor, and I could hear sirens over the splintering and roar of flames.

I shoved her through what was left of the front door and climbed out behind her just as my home caved in.

Someone grabbed me, then another person, and I was hoisted up and rushed away. The heat of the flames receded, and the cold night air filled my lungs. I started coughing violently, trying to get the smoke and soot out. I was led to an ambulance and sat in the back. They wanted to take me to the hospital.

"No," I said, waving a hand. "Where's the woman I came out with?"

"She's safe, sir. Don't worry," the EMT told me.

I was dazed and in need of oxygen, but otherwise I was alive. I found a mask over my nose and mouth, and I was instructed to breathe. They put a blanket over my shoulders, and someone was cleaning a cut on my forehead that hurt more than any other part of me.

The scene before me was a blurry disaster: lights flashing, people running, firefighters taking command of the scene. Even in the dark, it was too much for my eyes. I closed them and tilted my head down.

I took a few deep breaths and tried to understand what the fuck had happened, but my mind was racing. I was still so high on adrenaline; I couldn't think straight. All I remembered was calling Calvin.

Calvin.

I tugged the mask off, and the EMT ordered me to

put it back on. "Where's my boyfriend?" I demanded. It took a second for me to recall that Calvin hadn't been here.

But he was coming.

Or—

How long was I in the stairwell when everything first happened? Seconds? Or minutes? What if Calvin had gotten to the apartment when it exploded? I was having trouble remembering the chain of events properly.

"Sir, put the mask back on and breathe," the EMT said again.

"Sebastian!"

I looked up. I couldn't really see him, but I knew. "*Calvin.*" I shoved the blanket off and climbed out of the ambulance.

I didn't have to run blind all that far. Calvin grabbed me and locked his arms around me tight. I couldn't tell who was shaking. Maybe both of us.

But I started crying.

I gripped him so hard, it hurt. Chaos surrounded me, engulfed me, but my knight had come. He was there, and he held me, and I knew everything would be fine now.

"*Jesus fucking Christ.*" Calvin pulled his head back and kissed me with such force and desperation that I was gasping for air.

I felt his weight bear down on me, and I could feel his knees buckle. So I did what any prince was willing to do so that no one would see their knight's weakness. I took the fall. I dropped first, pulling Calvin down with me.

I could afford to look helpless. But no one could see that in him.

He was crying now too.

And we just held on to each other for a long time.

I don't remember how I got to Pop's that night, but considering my apartment no longer existed, his place was where I would have logically ended up. I was sitting on the couch, staring at the blurry entertainment system across the room. I remember it took me all damn day to install that furniture for my dad.

I am not Bob Vila.

Pop was sitting beside me on the couch, an arm wrapped around my shoulder. He dragged me down into a sideways hug, kissing the side of my head over and over.

Calvin stood nearby, doing something. Then he turned and held the something out in front of me. "Hey."

I blinked and shook my head, coming back to the moment. "What?"

"Your regular glasses were still in your jacket," Calvin said.

I reached out blindly, taking what he was holding and sliding the frames on. That was one minor crisis dealt with. On to my belongings, my home—Christ, I didn't even have a change of clothes.

Calvin went to the door and answered it when there was a forceful knock. I craned my neck, watching as Quinn entered with a big plastic bag in one hand. "Did you get everything?" he asked her.

"What I assumed was his. I stopped at the drugstore too. Toothbrush, razor, contact solution…."

"Thank you, Quinn."

She walked across the kitchen to the couch where Pop and I sat. "Sebastian."

"Quinn."

She set the bag down on the coffee table. "I picked up a few things for you. Some clothes you had at Calvin's, toiletries, you know."

"Oh."

She nodded and sat in the chair to the left of the couch.

"That was very kind of you, Ms.—?" Pop started.

"Quinn Lancaster. I'm Calvin's partner."

"I see."

There was more commotion then, the sound of several pairs of feet coming up the stairs to Pop's, but when I turned back to the door, Calvin opened it as if he were expecting visitors. Pop didn't budge from my side even as his place was soon filled with our two friendly detectives, a few uniformed officers, and an inspector with the FDNY whose name I didn't pay attention to. He looked kind of like Santa, though.

"Mr. Snow," Santa stated, looking directly at me.

"Huh?"

"Can I ask you a few questions?"

I nodded. At least, I think I did. I was so out of it and so fucking tired.

"Can you tell me where you were when the explosion went off?" Santa started.

"In the stairwell, I think."

"And prior to that, did you smell smoke? Gas?"

I don't remember smelling anything.

I realized I hadn't said that out loud when Calvin was standing at my other side once more and lightly touching my shoulder. "Seb," he prodded.

"Oh. N-no. No, I don't remember a smell."

"Did you see any suspicious individuals in the building?" one of the uniformed officers tried. "Or outside when you came home?"

I shook my head. "No. The building just—" I shrugged and raised my hands, as if that motion would explain it for me.

The interview was apparently over soon after that. I couldn't think of anything to say. I had no answers, no insights to help them. I could barely recall the entire incident myself. Calvin must have sensed that and known I was entirely useless. He talked with the officers while ushering them to the door, and I noticed too late that Quinn had gone as well.

Pop was standing then. "Is there anything else we can do tonight?"

"No," Calvin said.

I turned to look at Calvin and got to my feet. He still had his coat on, standing near the door, and his posture made him look uncomfortable. "Don't leave."

He hesitated.

"Pop, he can stay, right?"

"Of course he can."

Calvin's rigid stance eased. "Thank you." He slid his coat off.

Always polite. Waiting for permission.

Pop moved away from the couch and went toward his bedroom. "I'll make my bed up."

"Dad, I'm not taking your bed. I can sleep on the couch," I insisted, walking toward the kitchen and Calvin.

"Are you sure, kiddo?"

"Age before beauty."

Pop cracked a smile. "I'll get some extra pillows and blankets, then."

When he had vanished into the dimly lit room, arms slid around me and Calvin pressed against my body. I turned in his embrace and pressed my forehead against his shoulder. He had pulled himself together pretty quick after the moment we'd both had. But that was Calvin. He always bounced back fast, especially since he had to be seen as a commanding officer when Santa and his helpers were here.

Calvin let out a long breath and tugged his fingers lightly through my hair. "I promise you, I'm going to find who did this."

"I believe you."

"We'll talk about it tomorrow," he whispered, lips brushing the top of my head lightly.

"You don't have to be somewhere?"

"There's nothing I can do until the fire department finishes with the scene. Emergency response gets priority over your dead intruder."

"Dead intruder?" I echoed, before remembering.

Civil War.

Petticoat.

The blood on the floor.

I swore under my breath.

Calvin tightened his arms around me. "Shh. Later. We'll talk about it later."

And later it would be, because soon enough the apartment was dark and silent. Pop retired to bed, and Calvin and I squeezed onto the couch. Calvin was on his back and I was wedged on my side, half pressed against the back cushions and half laying on his chest.

Go figure, I was wide-awake now.

Wide-awake with such a level of exhaustion that it was prohibiting me from sleeping.

I held my cell, propping it up on Calvin's chest. I squinted and typed with one thumb—or rather, I tried, fumbling my way through the search phrase: *Bufglo blooc brck*.

I pulled my phone closer to read, squinting even against its decreased brightness.

Did you mean *Bologna Block brick?*

I grumbled and tried again.

Did you mean *Buffalo Block brick?*

Yes. Yes, I did.

I clicked the amended search and pulled up several websites about the history of bricks in America.

Calvin reached down, grabbed my phone, and leaned over to set it on the coffee table.

I tilted my head up to look at him. His eyes were closed. "Sorry."

He grunted.

"I can't sleep."

"I know. I can hear you thinking."

I put my head down on his chest and was lulled into a sort of peace by listening to Calvin's heartbeat. I ran my hand up and down his bare chest, slowing to enjoy the feel of chest hair between my fingers. Just the right amount. I moved to rub one of Calvin's nipples, and despite both of us being tired beyond belief, I was proud that his body reacted to such a small touch.

"Hey," he said, voice thick. "Not here."

I raised my head to look at his shadowed face. "Not into exhibitionism?"

"What?"

"Maggie."

Calvin turned his head, looking across the room at the dog bed, but Maggie was fast asleep, lying on her back with her paws lazily sticking up in the air. She snorted and snored peacefully. "I'm not fooling around on your father's couch, with him one room away."

"Reminds me of Ethan Cohen," I whispered.

"Reminds you—what?"

"My first hand job."

"On this couch?"

"Yep."

"With Ethan Cohen," Calvin stated.

"He was in twelfth grade. I was in eleventh."

"Let's not talk about someone else touching your dick."

"No reason to be jealous. He was terrible at it. Chafing."

Calvin snorted. He was trying not to laugh.

I smiled and put my head back down against him, tracing his nipple with my fingertip. "First and last time I had Ethan on this couch."

Calvin reached for my hand, raised it up, and gently kissed each finger. His warm, soft lips against my skin sent gentle currents of pleasure through me. "I'm glad it didn't work out." He kissed the inside of my wrist and nipped it lightly.

I shivered. I wanted to kiss Calvin. I wanted to kiss him more in that moment than I had in every second of our lives together so far. Sitting up, stuck between his arm and body, I leaned over and put my hand on his cheek. Tilting his face in my direction, I moved down to claim his mouth.

Like an Olympic athlete receiving the gold.

Victory was sweet.

CHAPTER FIVE

I woke up when I rolled off the couch and smacked the floor. "Son of a bitch," I muttered. A pillow fell down on my head and the blankets were twisted around my feet.

Maggie padded across the floor from nearby and snorted against the pillow.

"No," I told her, blindly putting my hand out to stop her vicious, slobbering tongue.

"You okay?" Calvin's inquiry was followed by calling for Maggie, who immediately left my side in his favor.

"Fine," I said against the floor.

"I'm making breakfast, kiddo," Pop called from a bit farther away. "Up and at 'em."

I sat up, groping around the coffee table for my glasses. When I could see, the living room was dim, curtains still closed against the oncoming morning. Dad was puttering around the kitchen, and Calvin was staring at me over the top of the couch.

"Did you sleep much?" Calvin asked.

I shrugged.

He nodded. So we were in agreement on that.

Quinn hadn't found the extra pair of pajamas I kept at Calvin's, so when I got up from the floor, I was wearing my underwear from yesterday and nothing else. I reached down, picked up the blanket, and wrapped myself up in it as Pop turned around.

He made a face, arm poised with a spoon covered in, I think, pancake batter. "Oh please. I was there the day your bare butt graced this world."

"Dad," I said firmly, feeling my cheeks get warm.

He motioned the spoon at Calvin. "Sebastian used to run around this house without a single piece of clothing on. Summer, winter, didn't matter. I was at wit's end trying to keep that boy in a pair of underwear."

"Okay. Good-bye," I announced, tugging the blanket as I moved from the couch to the hall. "I'm out when you start telling my boyfriend baby stories."

"You want some clothes?" Calvin offered.

He was grinning when I turned and took the bag that Quinn had brought over last night. When I got to the bathroom, I heard Pop start storytelling again and Calvin chuckle quietly.

Dropping the blanket, I hurried in and shut the door, went to the mirror, and grimaced. I was not winning any points for being an attractive man at that moment. I looked tired and had bags under my eyes. My hair was a mess, and some of it was still crusty with dried blood. I had a nice cut and bruise on my forehead, and I smelled like smoke, sweat, and sadness.

I looked at the counter. Quinn had picked me up solution and a container for my contacts, and that was so sweet. Calvin must have told her I wore them. And my new toothbrush still sat there from last night. I wish I could say *that* wasn't what tipped me over the edge, but I picked it up and stared at it and the tears started to well up.

Because this wasn't *my* toothbrush.

And this wasn't *my* home.

I sat on the edge of the tub, holding the brush and letting my head drop down as I tried to get a grip on myself. But it was hard. Because the toothbrush made me think of my bathroom, and the stupid shower curtain I bought when I first moved into the apartment. I had just graduated college, I was broke, had debts, and a shower that sprayed water everywhere without a curtain. First apartment purchase.

And that made me think of everything else.

Of the bed that Calvin and I lay in together, with the birds that chirped from the tall tree outside the window. Of the kitchen that Calvin enjoyed cooking in. The antique baking tools I had offered to keep from a recent estate sale, because he thought they were cool and wanted to use them. All of my books. My entire mystery collection—worn and loved with age and religious rereading. I thought of all the antiques that littered the place because I always figured, *I'll bring them to the Emporium tomorrow.*

Now there was no tomorrow.

I had lost all the stories behind those precious pieces of history.

I thought of my neighbor. Was Sally okay? What about the kids who lived above me? Had they been home, or were they at school when the explosion happened? The folks below me?

It hadn't just been me. There were eight apartments in the building. And they were all gone. It was such a good neighborhood. Who'd have done such a monstrous thing?

I knew it wasn't a gas explosion. I knew it from the

bottom of my heart. The destruction had originated either in my apartment or the one upstairs, because when I went to find Sally, I could remember the cold air. I was starting to recall those frantic, terrifying seconds once more. I hadn't seen the night sky—wasn't looking for it—but the air was vivid in my mind. My apartment had ceased to exist.

If that had been gas, I would have smelled it. So this meant… it had been intentional.

Had…? *Jesus*…. Someone had tried to kill me.

And not just pull a gun and be done with it.

They brought a building down on me. Talk about theatrics.

There was a gentle knock on the bathroom door. "Sweetie?" Calvin's muffled voice asked.

I looked up, sniffing and taking a breath. "Yeah," I called. "Sorry. I need to shower. I'll be out in a minute."

I hastily brushed my teeth, cleaned off under scalding-hot water, and popped in my contacts. After getting dressed in a pair of ratty Levi's and a likely white T-shirt from the bag, I wandered out of the steamy bathroom. "Pop," I called, entering the main room. "You don't still have that old electric razor somewhere, do you? Quinn got a manual for me, but I'm not drunk and confident enough to try it."

"Sorry, kiddo," Pop said. "We'll buy you one today."

Calvin came toward me then, nodding his chin at the bathroom. He'd already showered and dressed before I woke up. "I'll help."

"Help shave my face?"

"Sure."

"That seems weird."

"Barbers don't think so." He put his hands on my shoulders, turned me around, and walked me back. "Sit," he said, motioning to the toilet lid.

I sat and watched as Calvin grabbed a washcloth and warmed it under the hot water. He came over and pressed it against my face. "This is weird," I mumbled again.

Calvin didn't say anything. He smiled slightly and leaned over to press his lips to my forehead. Neither of us spoke. I stared at his face—all the freckles, his pretty hair. Those startling bright, gray eyes. Calvin's eyes betrayed his silence at times. In moments like this, when guards were down and there was a vulnerability between us, he let me see a lot of what was inside that didn't always make it out in words.

Love.

Affection.

Fear.

"I'm okay," I said through the washcloth.

He nodded. "I know. If anyone could troop through this, it'd be you, Seb."

I shook my head. "I'm just faking it until I make it."

"You're stronger than anyone I know." Calvin removed the washcloth after my face was sufficiently warmed up.

"Not you," I said as he grabbed shaving cream from the counter.

"Especially me." He turned and started rubbing my face with the soapy cream.

"I don't know what I'm going to do," I said before closing my mouth as he wiped my lips clean.

"You've got me and your father."

"I can't live on Pop's couch. And I can't crash with you forever. That… that stupid apartment was rent-controlled. I could walk to work. I hate the fucking trains. I don't want to deal with that twice a day. The lights hurt my eyes."

Calvin washed his hands and took the razor from

the bag I had left. He pulled it out of the packaging, ran it under the tap, and then turned back to me. "We'll figure something out," he said with a tone of finality.

So I didn't argue anymore.

Not that I had any intention of continuing while he had a sharp point against me.

Calvin held my face with a sure, steady hand, using gentle, deliberate strokes as he shaved. It was definitely strange, but I don't know…. There's something so tender and precious in these moments I had with him. The little domestic blisses. Blisses that made Calvin relax, that made me think everything *would* be okay in the long run— blisses that so many couples tried for and never achieved.

Accepted silence.

No walls.

Unconditional love.

"I like you a lot," I whispered as he rinsed the razor head. "Have I said that lately?"

Calvin's mouth quirked into a little smile. "I like you a lot too." And that was that.

He finished and stepped aside so I could wash my face.

"Wow, silky smooth," I said, touching my cheek. "And not even a tiny cut. You're good."

"Seb?"

I dried my face and looked up. "What?"

"Will you be able to come to the precinct so we can talk about last night?"

I swallowed as the image of the dead man bubbled up in my mind, but I nodded and squared my shoulders. "Yup."

Calvin set a hand under my chin, tilting it up. "You're my prince."

My heart slugged hard against my chest. I'd told Pop back at Christmastime that Calvin treated me different than any other guy I'd been with. Treated me like a prince. It was startling to hear him say what I had secretly entertained about the two of us.

Prince and Knight.

"And I will always protect you," he finished. "You know that, right?"

I swallowed the baseball-sized lump in my throat. "Sure do," I managed, trying to smile lightly. "You are my knight, after all."

That made him smile in return.

I kissed Calvin before walking to the door. "Come on," I said, clearing my throat. "I'm starving."

"How'd you manage?" Pop asked as we entered the room.

"There were no Sweeney Todd reenactments," I answered, going to the cabinets and helping him.

"Charming," Calvin said from behind me.

My dad snorted and started putting pancakes and bacon on the plates. I carried them to the table near the windows, set them down, and shooed Maggie away. She joined Calvin's side in the kitchen as he poured coffee for each of us. She sat obediently beside him, leaning lightly against his leg.

"She really likes you," I said.

Calvin looked down and nodded, then patted her head. "She's a good girl."

Pop watched them briefly before accepting the mug Calvin handed him. "Dogs are great for helping with stress." He gave me a look as he went by and sat at the table.

I had told Dad a little about Calvin's PTSD. I didn't know who else to talk to about it, and I needed someone to know because of how much I worried for his mental health. I'm not sure what Pop was thinking, but he had definitely, casually, suggested Calvin get a dog.

Luckily, I don't think Calvin really noticed the hint. Or at least didn't catch on as to why. I knew he'd be livid if he found out I was telling people—even if it was my own father—about his scars from war.

Calvin's cell rang and he paused what he was doing to pull it from his pocket. I watched him hesitate as he stared at the caller ID. His posture seemed to stiffen as he answered.

"Good morning, sir," he said quietly.

Sir? Maybe it was his sergeant.

Calvin said nothing at first—partaking in a one-sided conversation for a good minute. "Will he be released from the hospital?" he finally asked.

Who?

"I can't," Calvin answered. "I'm on a big case—"

I made a face. So definitely not his sergeant. His boss would kind of know what Calvin was doing, after all.

"My boyfriend's apartment burned down last night," he said, tone as if he were interrupting the person on the other line. After a beat, Calvin pulled his phone from his ear and stared at the screen. He shook his head and put it away.

I glanced at Pop behind me, who looked just as curious as I felt, before asking, "Wrong number?"

"No." Calvin turned from the counter and handed me a cup of coffee.

"I jest."

Calvin didn't smile. "That was my father."

I moved in front of him so Calvin couldn't walk. "Wait. Did he hang up on you? Why the hell did he even bother calling?"

To my knowledge, the man hadn't spoken to Calvin since Christmas. In fact, no father, no mother, no brother or sister. I mean, I knew they had an estranged relationship to begin with, but who the fuck calls their son and then *hangs up* on them?

"Because you mentioned me?" I asked.

"Don't worry about it, sweetie."

"What did he want?" I tried, still not moving. I couldn't be faulted for wanting to know.

Calvin glanced over my shoulder at Pop before looking at me again. "My uncle's health has been failing the past year. My father was updating me."

"Oh." And then I kind of felt like a shit, even though I hadn't been the reason his uncle was sick. "I'm sorry."

"He's being released from the hospital. He's a tough old guy."

"So did your dad want you to—go see him?"

Calvin just looked at me for another moment before reaching to rub my arm. "Come sit down." He nudged me toward the table.

Pop gave us both a smile as we sat. "I must say, I don't hear many kids referring to their father as 'sir' these days," he said lightly. "Reminds me of my old man."

"He's military. Retired colonel."

"Runs in the family, then?"

Calvin nodded. He took a big bite of food to stop the conversation.

In my head I had this mental picture of the sort of man Calvin's father was. Old, strict, likely disappointed in his hero of a son. After all, Calvin left the military as a major, which I knew was a notch or two in the belt below colonel. And *clearly*, gay was not okay in the Winter household. All it took was one little mention of me and his father ditched the call. I mean, fuck—I doubted the man even knew my name.

It made me feel weird, being hated by a guy who hadn't even met me.

But I'm sure it made Calvin feel like garbage.

Pop reached over and put a hand on Calvin's shoulder, giving him a firm pat. "You're always welcome in this house, understand?"

Calvin looked at Pop and nodded.

"And if you ever need anything, just ask."

Again, Calvin nodded. "Appreciate that."

Pop smiled and started eating breakfast.

I caught his look across the table and mouthed, "thank you," to which he winked. I don't know how I lucked out with a dad like mine.

I reached under the table and patted Calvin's thigh. He initially jumped at my touch, but immediately the muscles in his leg eased. A comfortable hush fell over the three of us after that.

Knowing that within the next few hours, Calvin would be expecting me to recount the details of my intruder turned dead man, I figured I should get my story straight before then. What had happened first? I walked home. Unlocked the front door, checked my mailbox, and went upstairs. I didn't bump into anyone on the stairs—Sally. Sally had been unlocking her apartment. She asked about Calvin, went inside, and I went into my apartment.

And then the guy was lying on the floor. He'd been on his stomach, and then I pushed him over and there was blood on the floor and his chest. Whether he'd been shot or stabbed, I didn't know. I hadn't thought to pay that much attention to the wound. Besides, it had been his clothing that surprised me.

That's right! He'd been wearing an old-fashioned petticoat.

I remembered thinking "Civil War," and I couldn't make sense as to why.

Something about his hair and funky little beard. It was just a style reminiscent of long ago. Like classic movie stars. People simply didn't look like that these days.

I took a sip of coffee.

The bricks and the dead guy were related events, for sure, but antique bricks and a Civil War general—

"Wait a minute," I heard myself say out loud.

Not a general.

A president.

"Wait?" Calvin asked, glancing up from his breakfast.

I looked at him and Pop before getting to my feet and going to the coffee table. "The guy. In my apartment." I came back with my phone to see Calvin poised for standing. "I remembered thinking he reminded me of, like, a Civil War soldier or something close to it, and I couldn't quite put my finger on why."

"Okay." Calvin stared, waiting for me to continue.

I held my phone close to type into the web browser. "He looked like this." I turned the phone around and held it out.

Calvin took it, staring at the screen.

"That's the former Confederate President, Jefferson Davis."

"Jefferson Davis died in your apartment?"

"Someone who could have been his brother did."

"I'm not following, Sebastian."

I took the phone back and typed again. "There's a story that Davis tried to escape Union troops by dressing as a woman. But—shit—" My typos were confusing the hell out of Google. "But it got exaggerated by the newspapers at the time. The real story is that he accidently grabbed his wife's coat instead of his own."

I handed Calvin the phone again when I had found pictures of northern newspapers from the time. Davis was comically drawn wearing a woman's skirt and undergarments, running through the woods.

I pointed at it. "The guy, last night? He was wearing a petticoat. Someone had put him in 1800s women's clothing."

"How can you be certain the clothes weren't his own?" Calvin asked.

Cop mode, activate!

"They weren't," I insisted. "I swear, if I still had a home, I'd bet on it that this guy was made to look like Davis from these newspapers. His hair was right, he even had that ugly little beard. So… you can use his picture as a model for who the dead man was."

"Good grief, Sebastian," Pop muttered, having stopped eating. He was staring at us both. "What have you gotten yourself into this time?"

I looked cool in aviator sunglasses.

Pop had found an old pair of prescription sunglasses that were mine once upon a time in a drawer. Why had I not kept this style? Maybe only *I* thought I looked cool.

I was sitting in the passenger seat of Calvin's car as he drove to the precinct. The dreary morning crawled by during rush hour.

Calvin turned the wipers on. "I'd rather have more of that epic snowstorm than this freezing rain," he murmured.

Agreed. This was the sort of cold, biting rain that made your soul shiver. At least the snow was pretty. It was mostly melted now, piles shoveled on street corners here and there, looking more like dirty blocks of ice than anything.

Calvin's hand touched mine.

I glanced at him and wove our fingers together.

I take what life gives me without much trouble. I think I've always been this way. Relaxed and composed to the point of it being suspicious. Hysterics get you nowhere. I see it as a waste of time and energy when you could instead take a deep breath and apply logic to your problem.

Not that I don't get upset now and then.

And I definitely had cause for that now, but really— it wouldn't have helped. I was homeless, but I had a loving boyfriend and father who would make sure I wasn't actually without a roof over me. I had no possessions, but besides society possibly frowning over me running around naked, they were just things. Things that made me happy, of course, but my building had blown up and I had walked away with only a cut and a bump on the head.

I was afraid to ask if all my neighbors had been so lucky.

"You should get a dog," I stated when Calvin put his hand back on the wheel.

"What?"

"A dog. I bet Pop would help pick out a good one."

"I'm too busy for a dog, Sebastian."

"Well… maybe you'd be inclined to take one less case or two if you had a pup."

"It doesn't really work that way," Calvin replied.

"Quinn said you've just been doing cold case work lately."

"That doesn't make them any less important. Maybe they're even more so. Justice has yet to be served."

"Man, you've got a heart of gold." I met Calvin's

expression, and he gave me a cute, sort of shy smile. "I can help take care of the dog too."

Calvin was quiet for a moment. He drove around a taxi and stopped at the next red light. "If we were living together?" he finally asked.

Er… was that what I had suggested? The idea of waking up beside Calvin every morning definitely made me excited.

"Snow and Winter—it's destiny," I joked instead, because I didn't want to make Calvin uncomfortable and it was way too early in our relationship to consider this huge step. "Can't you see our mailbox now?"

He smiled a little.

I waved my hand. "Not anytime soon."

"Yeah."

I dropped the dog and mailbox conversation.

Calvin managed to snag an open parking spot on the side of the road when we reached the precinct, and parallel parked like a goddamn wizard.

I whistled as he turned off the car and we got out. "Show off."

He laughed quietly. "Don't be jealous. You get to be chauffeured everywhere."

"True. It's great," I agreed, following him onto the sidewalk and toward the door where a few uniformed officers mingled.

They nodded at Calvin and shared a brief good morning. He opened the door and let me walk in first, then followed. Getting to bypass that same, less-than-chipper woman I had met in December was great. Although she did offer a glare that I suspected was as close as she got to saying hello.

We got into the elevator alone and Calvin pressed the button for his floor. After the doors closed, he reached out, took my hand, and gave it a brief squeeze. The warm strength of Calvin's touch was like silent love and assurance.

"You look good in those shades," he said as the doors opened and he dropped his hand.

"Yeah? All I need is a dramatic line to say every time I put them on."

I followed Calvin down a short hall and turned to walk through the open space of desks and detectives who were either early risers or hadn't yet gone home from the night before. Calvin made for another hall, unlocked his office, and ushered me inside. He left the light off, because he's a sweetheart, and hung up his jacket.

"So," he began, opening the window blinds enough for gray light to come in. "Sit down. Let's talk about Jefferson Davis."

"Don't interrogate me," I warned, unbuttoning my coat as I sat in the chair across from Calvin at his desk.

"You'd be in a smaller and more uncomfortable room if I were doing that."

"Remember that time you offered to book me and strip me?"

"Behave."

I grinned.

He took a moment to shuffle some papers and folders around before picking up a pen and filling out a form. "What time did you get home?"

I tugged my phone out of my pocket and checked the time I had called Calvin in a panic. "I called you at 7:18. So just a few minutes before."

"Tell me what happened after you walked in the front door of the building."

"Checked my mail—"

"Anything?"

"Preapproved credit cards?"

"Go on."

"Went upstairs, talked to my neighbor for twenty seconds, and went inside."

"The door was locked?"

I nodded. As a matter of fact, I had had the lock on my apartment changed after Christmas. So a whole lot of good that had done. "Yeah. Nothing seemed weird. But there he was, just lying on the floor."

"Where, exactly?"

"Beside the couch. On his stomach."

Calvin was writing as I talked. "Then what?"

"Umm… I shut the door. And… then I checked the guy."

"That was dangerous."

"I had a dictionary."

"What?"

I shook my head. "Never mind."

"Did you touch anything?"

"Can you lift fingerprints off soot and embers?"

"Don't be smart, Sebastian."

"I touched Davis. I mean, he didn't appear to be breathing, so I pushed him onto his back." I touched my chest as I spoke. "He had blood here. And on the floor."

Calvin glanced up. "Was it fresh?"

"I—I don't think so, not entirely. He wasn't stiff, so if rigor had set in, it hadn't gotten further than his face."

Calvin stared.

"So that makes it as early as one or two, most likely, though, around four or five yesterday evening that he was killed." I waved my hand while talking. "And you know, he couldn't have been alone."

"Why do you say that?"

"It's not like someone shot him and then carried a dead guy into my building, up three flights, and deposited him in my place. So if at least one person was with him, he would have been killed while they were inside. I don't think it was a knife wound, but if he were shot, the killer would have used a silencer, right? I have neighbors all on different schedules—someone would have heard and reported a gunshot."

Calvin set his pen down and stared at me.

"And unless he was deranged, he definitely didn't offer to be some sick sacrifice, so he trusted the person he was with. Nothing in my apartment was out of place, so no struggle."

Calvin grunted.

"And I guess the killer brought those clothes with them. The petticoat, I mean. Killed the guy, dressed him...." I frowned and tapped my chin. "But if nothing was stolen or ransacked—this was definitely deliberate. Do you think someone was trying to frame me?"

"I don't know, Sherlock."

"What?"

"You finished solving this case for me, yet?"

"Now who's being a smartass?"

"Can you think of any reason he was dressed and staged to look like Jefferson Davis?"

"Confederate sympathizers?" I asked with a shrug. "I really have no idea."

Calvin picked up his pen again. "You told the fire inspector last night that you didn't smell smoke or gas before the explosion. Are you certain?"

"Yeah."

Calvin nodded and wrote. "I got a call while you were in the shower. Gas company confirms it wasn't a leak. The inspectors believe some sort of homemade device set off the explosion."

"A bomb?"

"Yes. Three bodies were recovered," Calvin said. "It's a homicide case now."

"Jesus." I put a hand over my mouth.

"I have to confirm now if the bodies found were all tenants or if one was your intruder."

I nodded weakly. Sally and I had walked away. We were still breathing. We still had lives to live, people to love, jobs to work.

"I think it came from around my floor or the fourth," I whispered. "When I—I was in the hallway and I heard my neighbor, so I went to help, and I could feel cold air."

Calvin only nodded in agreement. "Do you need a glass of water?" he asked after a beat.

I shook my head. "I'm okay."

"Is there anything else you can tell me that might help?"

I started to say no but stopped. The note. "Shit. The note. There was another note," I said quickly. "The same paper and handwriting as the two I got at the Emporium."

Without moving a muscle, Calvin's entire demeanor changed. "What did it say?"

"Umm…. 'It started with a fire.'"

"Did you keep the note?"

"No. Sorry. I dropped it."

"But you have the other two?"

"Yes."

"'I know you like mysteries.' That was the first, correct?" Calvin asked.

"And the second said, 'Curious?'"

Calvin rubbed his jaw. "I need you to do something for me, Seb, and don't argue."

"I can't promise the second one."

"Keep the Emporium closed today."

"I have rent to pay. I can't stay closed."

"No. You need to," Calvin responded. "Because someone is singling you out. The first note was vandalism. The second was trespassing, the third was attempted murder. I don't want you alone in places where this person knows to find you."

Fuck me, this wasn't exactly easy to argue against.

"What am I supposed to do, then?" I asked. "Hire a tough guy named Bubba to be my muscle?"

"Lay low. Stay with your father," Calvin said.

"Calvin—"

"I said not to argue."

"And I said I couldn't promise that."

Calvin frowned. "If I could afford to stay with you instead, I would. But I'm on this case now, and I want to solve it fast. And I'll be able to focus if I know you are somewhere safe. Please do this for me."

I huffed and slumped in the chair, staring at the ceiling. "God, you do such a good guilt trip. If you weren't so cute, I'd ignore you."

"Glad to hear my freckles have such sway."

I snorted and looked back at Calvin. "You've been hanging around me too much."

"Probably."

I smiled. "Can I go, then, Detective? Or do I need someone to walk me home?"

Calvin sat up and pulled his wallet from his back pocket. He took out a few bills and handed them over. "Take a cab back."

"I have money."

"Seb—"

"Fine. Fine, fine." I took the money and shoved it into my coat pocket. "I'm just going to use it to buy cupcakes and whiskey, though. You can find me at Pop's between the hours of now and forever. I'll be drunk under a blanket, watching television."

"Atta boy."

I did hail a cab, but I had the guy drive to my street instead. Or as close as he could, considering the number of vehicles and people and roped off areas. I paid him and climbed out. I walked through the crowds that gathered to watch as the fire department finished dousing the remains of my building with water, while others combed through the debris.

I stopped at the line of tape that kept civilians at a safe distance. There was no structure left. The entire building had collapsed into a pile of dark rubble. It was surreal as hell.

"Did everyone make it out?" someone asked from behind me.

"I don't know," a second said.

"Oh, I heard on the news this morning that some bodies were found," a third voice chimed in.

"How awful," the first answered.

I felt my stomach roll. Whether I was friendly with my neighbors, or even knew their names, wasn't the point. Someone had made a threat and attack against me, and others had suffered as a result.

Others had died.

Not me.

I dug my fingers into my palms, nails biting the flesh. It made me angry. Really, *really* fucking angry. But like how I dealt with the rest of life's curveballs, I took a breath. Because lashing out blindly wasn't going to do shit. But finding out who did this? Sending them to jail where they belonged? Giving closure to the families, like Calvin did for his cold cases?

That was how I was going to channel this rage.

I had a knack for encouraging the unstable to latch on to me. Just as in December, this was personal, and I wasn't going to let it rest. If I really was the cat curiosity tried to kill, I figured it had only gotten one or two of my lives so far. Plenty left.

There was a mystery afoot.

So much for my cupcakes and whiskey.

CHAPTER SIX

I stepped away from the crowd and my former home when my phone started ringing. I held it close to see Max's name on the caller ID. "I didn't call you," I said upon answering. "I'm so sorry."

"You're alive!" he shouted. "Oh my God. I saw on the news this morning. Seb, what happened?"

"It's a long story."

"But that was your apartment building, wasn't it?"

"Yes."

"Holy shit. *Holy shit*," Max cried. "Was it a gas explosion?"

I hesitated. I didn't want to worry him more than necessary. "Maybe. They're still investigating," I lied.

Max groaned. "Where are you staying? With Calvin?"

"My dad's right now."

"Do you need anything?"

"No, I'm okay. But thank you."

"What about the Emporium? Do you—I can run it alone if you need."

"I'm going to stay closed for a day or two," I answered. "Your pay won't be affected."

"I don't care about that."

Sweet kid.

I had taken another step and was just about to tell Max once more that I was really okay, because the poor guy sounded more shaken than I did, when something hit my foot hard. "Ouch! Son of a bitch," I muttered, looking down.

"What? You okay?" Max's voice echoed.

"Yeah, fine—" I stared down at a brick beside my foot.

I whipped my head up and looked around, but no one seemed to be paying me any notice. Uniformed personnel walked about, and civilians were all still watching the scene behind me.

"Max, I have to go. I'll call you later. Thank you again. I mean it."

"Sure, Seb. Be safe, all right? Do you know how hard it'll be to find another boss with your level of sarcasm and crotchety behavior? One doesn't just stumble onto that every day."

"You're too kind." I said good-bye and hung up.

I looked down at the brick again before crouching to examine it. Antique, similar to the ones in the Emporium, with a rubber band and slip of paper. I swallowed and pulled it free. Unfolding the note carefully at the corners, I squinted to read the message.

He lost the whales but not the mermaid.

Below that was an address on the Upper West Side. I frowned and read it again. He lost the whales? Who was *he*? What mermaid? I couldn't make sense of the message, but I knew the address.

"Museum of Natural History," I murmured.

I should have called Calvin.

But going to the museum wasn't dangerous. And really, I was only looking around. It's not like they had mermaids on display, so what was I even doing there? What did the clue mean?

No big deal.

But as I raced up the steps, past the statue of Theodore Roosevelt, it struck me suddenly that the museum *did* have a whale display. A *massive* whale. It was a ninety-four-foot-long model of a blue whale that hung suspended from the huge Hall of Ocean Life. What did that mean, though?

Was there going to be another clue waiting for me?

This was like some sort of fucked-up treasure hunt. Would a dead body be my *X* that marks the spot?

Damn it, I really should have called Calvin.

But now I was too wrapped up in seeing where this led. I couldn't walk away. Not yet. Calling him was logical, of course. He was a cop; he was working with the fire investigators and would undoubtedly solve the murder and find out who tried to off me. But he was also my boyfriend, and call it some stupid macho-man thing, but I felt like a damsel in distress with my default to chaos being to call Calvin.

I could handle this.

And I'd tell him what I learned.

I stood at one of the kiosks in the main entrance, holding my magnifying glass to the screen as I fumbled through ticket options. One adult ticket, no special exhibits. I swiped my credit card and waited for the stub to be dispensed from the machine.

I needed to take a moment and step back from the clusterfuck of a situation I was in. The past two days had been such a whirlwind of insanity, I was now knee-deep in shit on Thursday morning, at the Museum of Natural History, with next to no understanding as to why.

The kiosk spit my ticket out.

I looked down, grabbed it, and left the fairly empty lobby to step into the next hall. I moved to the display on the wall that featured photos of each exhibit and where they were located—after all, the museum was multiple floors and you had to plan your visit because there was no way you'd see it all in one day. I tapped the picture of the whale. I made my way toward the Hall of Biodiversity, which I had to walk through to reach the marine life. And with each step, I laid out my clues.

Start with the obvious. What were the facts so far?

Tuesday morning someone threw an antique brick into my shop. The message was direct and definitely written for me. Someone knew I had a compulsion to solve mysteries. Wednesday someone broke into my shop and filled it full of the same bricks. The second note had solidified my interest in what was happening, egging me on to begin subtle investigations of my own.

And then there was the body. I didn't know who he was or why he was presented in such a manner, but it was a glaringly obvious clue I wasn't quite putting into place. And the message.

It started with a fire.

But that didn't imply my fire, did it? I felt like it was a message about a past event. And this newest one now—I had been handed more clues than I knew how to process.

He lost whales. In… a fire? And Jefferson Davis?

I shook my head and waved the clutter away from my mind.

The fact that someone gave me a clue this morning was *really* the reason I should have called Calvin. No one knew I was going to the scene of my former home. Pop knew I went to the precinct, Calvin thought I was going home, and I didn't tell Max where I had been when he rang. So had someone followed me? From the precinct? From *Pop's*?

That didn't sit well.

At least I knew he was out for the day at his shelters, and Maggie was a good guard dog who wouldn't let anyone she didn't trust near my dad.

I couldn't shake the idea that whoever this was could be someone I was familiar with. It had to be. Knowing what made me tick, where I lived, where to find me.... I'm not on all of the hip social media sites that kids are on. I don't advertise myself to creeps online. So it had to be someone in my life.

But who did that leave? If I gathered up all the folks who knew me well enough into a drawing room to name the culprit, I'd be left with Pop, Calvin, Max, Beth, and I guess Neil. Yeah. All *real serious* suspects.

I know you like mysteries.

Uh-huh. And this one was a stumper.

The Hall of Biodiversity was much dimmer than the lobby and a relief for my eyes. I had to resist the natural urge to stop and look at displays or watch videos, instead making a direct line for the next hall. And there was the great whale, greeting me as I walked in. The behemoth towered over the two-story room, looking down at visitors and displays with all of its twenty-one thousand pounds.

All right. So here was the whale. I looked left and right.

No dead bodies. A plus, I supposed.

I took the stairs down to the ground floor, walking

under the whale and looking up in awe like every kid and adult always does. There were few people in the room with me, since it was just after opening at the museum and I hadn't been sidetracked by the other halls first. I walked along the wall, taking a brief moment to study the displays of dolphins, walruses, fish, and all other crazy forms of sea life.

I found myself also looking over my shoulder—because so far my clues were usually *thrown at me*. I not only wanted to see who was doing this and tackle the motherfucker to the ground, but I didn't want to get beaned in the head with a brick either. But there was no one. Two people were watching the video on deep-sea submersibles while standing under the whale. A few more lingered on the floor above, making a slow circuit around the room.

No one was following me. No one was watching me.

Had I made a mistake?

I didn't feel like it.

I huffed and walked back to stand under the whale, staring up at it. Maybe it had implied a different whale display, although for the life of me, I couldn't think of where else in this museum that would be. And there weren't any special, limited exhibitions going on that had anything to do with either whales or mermaids.

And really, what the hell was the mermaid comment supposed to mean? This was a museum of *science*. Mermaids were folklore. Myths, art, scams—

My thoughts came to an abrupt stop as I looked toward the far left. The corner was darker, and I'd definitely forgotten about the display, but there it was. The squid and the sperm whale. Or rather, the squid and the head of the sperm whale, because the model was huge.

I immediately walked in that direction, approaching it head-on. The squid was caught in the whale's mouth, fighting valiantly. And there, on the stand with information on the exhibit, was a newspaper clipping.

It was in a plastic sheet and taped over the sperm whale description. I looked around once more, but there was no one watching me. Pulling out my magnifying glass again, I pried the sheet free and held it up close.

The newspaper was dated January 1843. *Charleston Courier*. It featured a bare-breasted mermaid and advertised a most wonderful curiosity! Only fifty cents to view the mermaid, which with inflation was somewhere around fifteen dollars these days. That was a hell of a lot of money to see a dried-out, dead monkey sewn to a fish tail.

Wait.

I was thinking of the Feejee Mermaid.

But that's what this was, wasn't it? This was one of the original ads for the mermaid that P.T. Barnum had boasted as part of his collection of curiosities. In fact, if memory served me right, it was one of his best business hoaxes. A naturalist from England, who was actually not a naturalist at all but hired by Barnum to pretend, had brought to America a most interesting oddity found in the South Pacific. Barnum had orchestrated "Dr. Griffin's" arrival, excited the newspapers with false advertising of seductive mermaids, and borrowed a very fake, gross-looking thing that crowds believed to be a hideous mermaid.

And whether spectators accepted it as truth or not wasn't the point. Barnum had so successfully played on human curiosity that everyone wanted to see the creature for themselves. I believe I read somewhere that ticket sales to his museum skyrocketed while the mermaid was "on loan" from Dr. Griffin.

So, was this my clue? An old newspaper clipping?

I turned it around, and there was a note taped to the back of the plastic sheet.

Prove the murder, win a mermaid!

What. The. Fuck.

My hands were sweaty and my gut churned uncomfortably. This was like some macabre carnival, where instead of popping the balloons and winning a teddy bear, I had to solve gruesome deaths to win a mummified animal. But what murder was the note referring to? Jefferson Davis 2.0?

"Kind of hard to solve when you fucking blew him up," I growled at the note.

I had nearly turned away from the display, angry and frustrated and kind of scared, before I noticed *something* from the corner of my eye. It was in the exhibit with the whale head and squid. I took a few steps closer and leaned in, looking into the dimness.

Sparkly stiletto shoes.

A glittery purse and shimmering dress.

There was a dead woman lying on the floor.

"Fuck me," I whispered.

No panicking this time!

I swallowed and got closer still. Her dress was tight and looked like something you'd wear to a club, not a museum. And I especially couldn't imagine walking around this massive building in four-inch heels. So I came to the logical conclusion that she had not been here to patronize the museum.

She appeared a bit older than me. Maybe early forties, but she looked fit and well-built, like a frequent flyer at a gym. Her hair was long and pale—I guessed it was what I assume blonde was. I quickly set the newspaper clipping down on the floor and pulled my jacket sleeve over one hand before reaching into the display and lifting her hand.

It was rigid and difficult to move. Rigor had been set for a while—

perhaps she had been killed last night? I held up

my magnifying glass and examined her hand. She had long, shimmering nails that matched the rest of her attire. I tugged the hand over and looked under the nails, but I didn't see anything suspicious. I dropped it and moved the magnifying glass up to see the dark spot in the middle of her chest.

"Shit."

Same wound as my intruder. Shot point-blank? In a public space, no less. And then shoved into a display to not be seen by anyone yet, likely only because it was in a dark corner and there were more interesting exhibits elsewhere.

I gave her purse a glance.

Don't touch, I told myself.

So naturally, I touched it.

It was a dumb little thing, not big enough to hold anything important. It had a snap on top, but it was already undone, so I simply tugged it open. Three tampons, a wad of cash, and what looked like a few business cards. I carefully pulled one free, holding it by the corner and turning it around to read.

Ricky's Private Parties.

Ah-ha.

Exotic dancer, isn't that what they're called these days?

It explained the clothing she must have been freezing in. And the abundance of glitter.

1-800-GET-LAPS

Jesus, how classy.

I pulled out my cell and dialed the atrocious number, then listened to the ring.

"Ricky's Private Parties," said a less-than-interested-sounding girl upon answering.

"Uh, hi," I stated.

"Sorry, sir. Ricky's is closed right now. You can book a private event on our website. Otherwise call back this evening at—"

"Wait, I'm not trying to—I just have a question. It's about one of your dancers."

"You can see our dancers' bios on the website."

"Hold on," I said more firmly. "I wanted to ask about a—er, blonde woman." I glanced at the lady, and against the queasiness in my stomach, I leaned in to press my hand against her neck and chest.

Cold.

But definitely stiff.

She'd been dead a while, then. At least twelve hours, if not more, to account for the fact that the museum closes just before six and she would have had to have been brought here. So maybe she never went to work last night.

"I, uh—came to see her perform yesterday, but she never showed up and I was worried."

"Meredith—I mean, Crystal?" she asked suddenly.

Score. Dancer name, Crystal; real name, Meredith.

"Will she be in today?" I asked lamely. I'd never even been interested in watching male strippers, let alone women. Not my style.

"Oh, maybe. Umm, I think she may be sick," the girl said, clearly not sure and doing her best to hide concern. "Try calling tonight."

"Okay, thank you." I hung up, then chose Calvin in my contacts. "Before you get all Bad Cop, sexy alpha on me," I said just as Calvin said hello, "just know that this shit follows me. I did not seek it out…. Not really, anyway."

"What are you talking about?" Calvin asked.

I glanced down at Meredith. "I found another murder."

I'm the first person to understand that murder isn't great for business. So the fact that, before I knew it, museum security had ushered patrons out, suspicious old me had been forbidden to leave, and the director had escorted Calvin and Quinn across the massive room, more or less imploring the NYPD to make it quick and get the hell out, was not any surprise to me.

No one wants a dead exotic dancer to outshine the newest dinosaur exhibit.

Bad for donations, I imagine.

Calvin stopped several feet away from me, put a hand on his hip, and ushered me over with one snap of his wrist.

I stepped away from the nearby display I had been planted at while waiting. "I only found her," I said, reaching his side.

Calvin set both hands on his hips. "What did I tell you?" he whispered. "I told you to go to your father's. This is not there. What the hell are you doing here?"

"I got another note after leaving the precinct," I whispered back, rather loudly. "It had this address, so I decided to come. It's a public place—what was going to happen to me?"

"The same thing that happened to this woman," Calvin said.

"Well, it didn't," I answered stupidly, crossing my arms. "I'm fine."

Calvin pinched the bridge of his nose. "Sebastian, how did you not learn the first time? How many different ways do I have to tell you how suspicious you look in these situations?"

"Oh, please," I hissed. "She's been dead at least

twelve hours. I've got alibis for days."

"And if you keep popping up every time a dead person does, sooner or later you will be seen as a convenient suspect."

"I don't even know these people. I have no motive," I argued.

Calvin raised a finger to silence me. "Motive isn't important. One person's reason to kill may not be understood, but it was sound enough for them in the moment."

I groaned and dropped my head down. "For fuck's sake, Calvin. Fine. *My bad*, okay?"

"My bad?" he echoed, voice deep and very much not amused.

"Not the time or the place, gentlemen," Quinn finally said. "Calvin caught me up on all this shit," she continued, looking up at me. "What was this new note?"

I reached into my pocket and removed the paper. "I stopped on my street to see—everything. Someone threw a brick at me. And no, I didn't see who."

Quinn took the paper, and Calvin read it over her shoulder.

"With this address and the mention of the whale, I thought it must have been talking about that guy." I motioned above us. "But obviously I got here and there was nothing. I almost left until I remembered this display here. It's a sperm whale."

"Yes, fascinating," Quinn remarked.

"Sort of. Squids and sperm whales are—"

"Focus, Seb," Calvin muttered.

I huffed and turned to point at the display. "So I came over here and found a newspaper clipping." I held it up next. "It's an original, I think. It's one of P.T. Barnum's ads for his Feejee Mermaid."

"That's the second time you've mentioned Barnum," Quinn said.

"Uh, I guess that's true," I said when I recalled my mention of the bricks and the story of Barnum's unique advertising. "There's another note on the back." I turned it around for both detectives to see. "That's when I saw Meredith."

Calvin glanced up from the note, narrowing his eyes. "Meredith?"

"She goes by Crystal. A dancer, I think. I called the number on the business card in her purse."

Calvin took a breath and raised his hands, sort of like he wanted to strangle me, but Quinn took his jacket sleeve and tugged him away to look at the body.

I pulled my phone out once I was alone again. *I* was supposed to solve the murder. Not that I wanted to win a prize, but anything learned could bring us one step closer to catching a mistake this maniac made and taking them down before another person could be hurt. I pulled up the web browser and briefly checked out Ricky's online presence. Lots of scantily clad ladies and dubious use of Photoshop. It didn't look like anything particularly special—one gentlemen's club is like all the others.

I tried searching for any news related to the club. Maybe there was some dirt on the owner, or bad blood between rival businesses. If I lived anywhere else, I'd say that was ridiculous, that this poor woman just got jumped and the tragedy was that there was no reason for her death, but I live in New York City and last Christmas I was stalked by a guy who planted a heart under the floorboards of my store.

Anything is possible.

Nothing of any particular interest was showing up in Google's news feed for Ricky's, other than some *sizzling winter ball* they'd had in January.

I looked over at the group of police and a few museum personnel. Calvin had climbed into the display and was looking down at Meredith. I squinted—it was hard to see his expression from where I was. But Calvin had certain tics I had begun picking up on in his posture that helped me understand his mood when it was difficult to read his face. And I think he was surprised just then, because he had a hand over his mouth, rubbing his jaw.

That was interesting to me.

Did Calvin know her?

Not personally, of course. He might have been in the closet until recently, but I knew Calvin wasn't one for lap dances from ladies either.

Now *I* would certainly sit on his lap and show him a good time, but I drew the line at putting on glitter.

"Fuck," I murmured to myself, because now I had the image in my head of me naked, riding Calvin's cock, and having the *greatest* of times, and that was *so* not what I should be thinking about at a murder scene. "Get it together," I muttered.

I caught a uniformed officer glancing at me in confusion.

I squared my shoulders and took an extra second to look at Calvin as a professional, and not my unbelievably gorgeous boyfriend, which was admittedly a little hard to do. He was saying something to Quinn, who appeared to agree with him. Maybe Meredith had been on the wrong side of the law before. But if Calvin knew her, it had definitely been serious. A suspect in a murder case?

I looked down at my phone again and tried a few keywords that included Meredith, Ricky's, and murder. I found exactly what I was hoping for, third link down on the list.

NYC Exotic Dancer Suspect in Daughter's Death.

That didn't paint Meredith in a particularly good light. I clicked the link and expanded the page to better read the text. It was a case from two years ago, led by the recently promoted Detective Calvin Winter. DNA evidence had been incorrectly handled at the scene and was unusable in laboratory testing. Meredith's alibis had apparently been suspicious, but her boss had backed her statement, and Calvin had ultimately ended up with no legal way to prove she had bludgeoned her teen daughter to death.

"Calvin!" I called out, and when a few officers looked at me, I followed up with, "I mean, Detective Winter. Could you come here?"

Calvin got out of the display and walked toward me. "What?" he asked in a low tone.

I held out my phone. "This is the same lady, isn't it?"

He looked at the article. "Yes. How did you find this?"

I shrugged. "Seemed like she was familiar to you."

Calvin's mouth formed a tight line and he gave my phone back. "It's a cold case. Not enough evidence to convict her, but everyone knew she did it."

"The note said I had to prove the murder."

Calvin raised a hand to stop me. "No."

"But—"

"No. Stop right now, Seb."

"But what if it leads us one step closer to who did this? You're going to ignore that chance to stop this person?"

"I'm not, no. But you are."

"Like hell."

Calvin took a long breath. "We're not having this argument again. Plant your ass on your father's couch and stay out of trouble."

"It seems pretty suspicious to me that one of your cold case suspects was murdered," I said without regard to Calvin's statement. "What about someone seeking revenge? The daughter's father, maybe? A friend? Did the daughter have a boyfriend? Someone who would want to bring closure. Someone who clearly knew the mother was guilty."

"I know how to do my job," Calvin retorted.

"I didn't say you couldn't. I'm just trying to work this out."

"Sebastian, what's your degree in?" Calvin interrupted.

"My what?"

"Degree."

"Uh… fine art."

"Not criminal justice?"

"I get it," I stated, crossing my arms.

"No, you don't," he said before taking another breath. "Baby, I know you're smart. I know you've got a knack for figuring this shit out. You don't have to prove it to me."

"I'm not trying to—"

"This is dangerous. Do you not remember what happened last time?"

All too well, actually. And the guilt hit me like a truck out of control on a freeway. If Calvin ever got hurt again because of my own stupidity, I don't know what I'd do with myself.

It was painful to swallow. I stared at my shoes. "Sorry," I whispered.

"I only want you to be safe," Calvin said after a beat. "If—if your expertise were ever required for me to solve a case, I'd call on them."

That made me look up. "You would?"

"Yeah."

"Not that you expect to ever need someone skilled in trinkets from Victorian America to solve a murder."

"You helped with *Tamerlane*," Calvin pointed out.

"I guess."

"Seb, I don't want anyone questioning your involvement in this. You understand that, right?"

I nodded. I was done arguing. I hated fighting with him. I really did. I loved Calvin too much to bicker, especially when he was right and I was wrong and I knew that from the start.

But the urge to put the mystery to bed myself was still overwhelming. Maybe I did subconsciously crave some sort of way to prove I was smart. That I was clever. Useful, even. That what I did with my life made a difference, like Calvin's.

Jesus. I needed a hug or something.

"Can I wait at your place tonight?" I asked.

"I'm going to be working—"

"Come home," I insisted. "Please?"

Someone from behind called my name, and we both turned.

"N-Neil?" I heard myself stutter.

Neil stood a few feet away, holding a forensic kit in one hand.

"Why are you here?" he asked me.

"Uh… getting into trouble. Per usual."

Neil looked at Calvin. "Detective Winter," he said coolly.

"Millett," Calvin said with a nod.

This wasn't awkward at all.

What were the chances my ex would be the CSU

detective assigned to collect evidence?

Someone roll the week back to Monday. I demand a do-over.

I cleared my throat. "Has it gotten sufficiently uncomfortable?"

"Yes," Neil answered.

"Okay, good. I'm leaving now," I answered.

"I'll have an officer drive you," Calvin said. "To my place."

I caught the sour look that took over Neil's face. "Thanks," I answered.

CHAPTER SEVEN

I stood in front of the mirror in Calvin's bathroom, trying to fish my contact lens out from under my eyelid.

"Motherfucker," I growled.

That's what I got for crashing hard after I had been dropped off. I guess the poor sleep from the night before finally caught up with me. It was early evening when I woke up, and I was groggy, hungry, and searching for the mystical vanishing lens—

"Ah, finally!" I blinked a few times before putting my glasses on and checking myself in the mirror.

Hmm. Gray, grumpy, and gay. The Holy Trinity.

I stepped out of the tiny room and opened Calvin's fridge only a few steps away. Beers, a package of untouched strawberries, and something covered in plastic wrap that I think had been there two weeks ago when I'd last spent the night. Calvin was a wonderful cook—when he was actually home to toss something together. I took out my cell, pulled up a delivery app, and picked the first restaurant I came across.

Beef tongue sandwich?

Oh, hell no.

I kept scrolling.

Shawarma. That wasn't bad. I picked two, under the hopeful assumption Calvin was indeed coming home, and a few stuffed peppers before placing the order.

I gave Pop a ring next. "Hey-o, Daddy-o," I said when he answered.

"Hey-o, kiddo."

"I think I'm staying at Calvin's tonight. I just wanted to let you know."

"All right. How did the visit to the precinct go?"

"Fine. I successfully proved my innocence to Detective Winter, but it was touch-and-go for a while."

"Very funny."

"You never know. Maybe I tried to blow myself up."

"Sebastian."

"Have you seen my student loans?"

Pop cleared his throat.

"Sorry."

"Don't joke about that."

"It's my default."

"Yes, I know. Is Calvin home with you?"

"Not yet."

"Well, you call me if you need anything."

I nodded to myself. "I will. And Pop? You be careful too. Not that you're in danger!" I quickly amended. "Just… I love you."

"I love you too."

I said good-bye after, turned on the television, and

flopped back onto the bed on the opposite wall of Calvin's tiny studio. From the murmur of the voices, some reality Bigfoot show was playing. Super exciting stuff. I crossed my arms behind my head and glared at the ceiling.

P.T. Barnum.

Phineas Taylor Barnum. Died in 1891, if memory served me right. A famous showman and businessman, known not only for his hoaxes, but the curious, the bizarre, and even his role in the high culture of opera. He founded the Barnum & Bailey Circus, which was what most people likely knew his name from, but he also had a museum here in New York City—Barnum's American Museum—until it was destroyed in a devastating fire in 1865.

My breath caught.

The fire.

It started with a fire.

I sat straight up. Barnum's museum was a tragic loss. His actors survived, but countless animals perished, and the artifacts had all been lost, from the bizarre and worthless to significant and priceless. It was even rumored that was where the Feejee Mermaid vanished.

"Fuck me!" I grabbed my phone and opened the web browser.

The shit I retained. I swear to God….

I opened a page that detailed the events of July 13, quotes from newspapers of the times discussing the tragedy in their dated and extravagant language. Sure enough, after several minutes of reading and swiping through some photographs of Barnum's advertisements, I confirmed that he actually had live whales on display in the basement of the museum. When the fire started, scared staffers broke their tanks, hoping to douse the flames.

It didn't work.

And the poor whales were left to slowly die.

He lost the whales, but not the mermaid.

Was that what the morning's note was in regards to? Barnum's whales that perished in the fire? Did it imply the most famous hoax of Barnum's career, the mermaid that was thought lost forever, was still hanging around somewhere?

Prove the murder, win a mermaid!

I looked away from the phone and got to my feet. "Meredith Brown was a prime suspect two years ago in the murder of her teenage daughter," I said out loud. "But lost DNA evidence and a shaky alibi saved her." I shrugged. "I bet she was murdered to bring closure to her daughter. How am I supposed to prove Meredith was guilty when Calvin couldn't?"

Well… there was one difference between Calvin and I. He had laws and legal tape to work around. I was just a nosy prick. But how could I prove she committed murder two years after the fact?

Was my creepy new stalker going to give me the Feejee Mermaid as a reward if I managed to do just that?

The only glaring clue I had still been overlooking was Jefferson. So like the little detective I seemed to think I was, I started searching the internet again. I really should have done so sooner, too, because the answer was surprisingly easy to find. Some of the many lost items in Barnum's fire had been wax figures of famous and notorious individuals—Jefferson Davis in petticoats included. Apparently someone had thought to save it by tossing it out a window. When the wax figure landed on the street, the public—for whom the Civil War was a fresh wound not hardly healed—hung it from a nearby lamppost.

What Barnum had to do with any of these modern murders was beyond me.

I set my phone back down and took a breath. I wish the dead guy in my apartment hadn't been lost to the flames. His identity was important, I knew it, but what if they never found any of his remains?

My pondering was soon left behind when the front door buzzer rang. I let the delivery guy into the building and unlocked the apartment door as he was coming up the stairs. I took the bag of food, tipped the kid, and shut and locked the door again. I walked over to the kitchenette and started rummaging through the takeout. I hadn't gotten much further than debating whether to put Calvin's portion in the fridge for his inevitably late arrival, when the door was unlocked and said redhead walked in.

"Hey," I said, smiling when I turned to greet him. "You're home earlier than I—"

Calvin threw the dead bolt on the door, took three powerful strides toward me, and pulled me into a fierce kiss before I could finish speaking. I bumped against the counter, take-out bag crinkling loudly as I was pushed back. Calvin's hips pressed roughly against my own as he shoved his tongue in my mouth.

Jesus fuck!

I grabbed the front of his jacket and nearly tore the buttons loose while frantically trying to open it. I pushed it off his shoulders, listening to the heavy fabric fall to the floor with a quiet thump. Calvin broke the kiss, taking about half a second to remove his shoulder holster and shove the weapon onto the counter behind me. He grabbed my face in both hands and kissed me hard.

I swear I saw stars.

I pulled his hips forward once more, grinding against him. I had no idea what put him in this mood, because last I checked, murder wasn't exactly a turn-on, but I was more than ready to match his enthusiasm. He wanted it hard and rough, and so did I. Right here in the kitchen, on the floor—his studio didn't leave much to the imagination, but I wasn't picky.

Calvin shoved my T-shirt up, broke the kiss, and leaned down to bite and suck my nipple. I yelped and bumped back against the counter again. He grabbed me tight and held me in place, continuing to bite and suck until I couldn't take any more.

"C-Calvin!"

He straightened, his large frame engulfing me. "Beg me to fuck your ass," he whispered. Calvin wrapped a big hand around my throat.

I managed to swallow before he tightened his grasp. "Please."

"Please what?"

To hell with thinking I sounded lame. "Fuck me, make me come!"

Calvin grinned, his mouth hovering a kiss away from mine. "I'm going to shove you against the wall and pound your perfect ass until you can't walk, baby."

Holy hell.

And then we were kissing again while struggling to do away with each other's clothes. I liked giving Calvin a fight for dominance, even if I was in fact looking to be the one dominated, because it ignited a fire in him that was so unbelievably hot. I needed the roughness of his hands on my body, craved the words he spoke, but I loved that Calvin never once stopped caring for my well-being.

I'd lost my shirt and my jeans were unbuttoned and hanging off my hips when I was backed up against the wall beside the counter. I grabbed Calvin's tie, yanking him forward to kiss and grinning against his mouth when he growled in response.

He shoved my pants and boxer briefs down as we kissed, then reached behind to grab my ass firmly. "Gorgeous ass," he murmured when we broke the kiss for breath. Calvin dropped to his knees next. "And gorgeous dick." He took the head of my cock into his mouth, tightening his lips around me and sucking hard.

"Oh God," I groaned, hitting the back of my head against the wall. It was both too much and not enough. I needed more—needed Calvin fucking me, claiming me, making me hoarse from screaming as he screwed me senseless. I didn't want it to end yet.

Calvin's a very intuitive sexual partner. He seems to know what I want before I do, and he can pull me back from jumping off the ledge into a mind-numbing orgasm too soon. He can draw it out, make it something to write home about every time.

He took his mouth off me and finished helping me step out of my clothes. Then he turned me around, pushed me against the wall, spread my cheeks, and licked me.

I shivered in response. It was a freezing-hot feel. I was burning up from the inside out. Unable to get a grip on the wall, I pounded my fist against it in vain. "Cal," I groaned. "I can't take it, please!"

"What's wrong?" he asked, but there was a mischievous tone in his words.

"Stop teasing."

He stood behind me and smoothed his hands over my ass again, leaning in close. "You'll take it, and like it," he whispered in my ear before smacking one cheek hard.

He did it again and again. My skin tingled and stung in the most erotic and delicious way imaginable. I was vaguely aware of the inarticulate words I moaned against the wall being heard by Calvin's neighbors—but to hell with them. They could listen to me scream. I wasn't going to be quiet. They'd probably be jealous.

Calvin moved away, and I turned my head to look back, watching him strip out of his suit and show me the muscular body that hid underneath. *Fuck*, he was so goddamn stunning. Pale skin, constellations of freckles upon freckles, and just enough light-colored hair in all the places that I liked it. Not even the multiple scars of bullet wounds detracted from his beauty.

He walked to the bed, opened the drawer of the nightstand, and rummaged about before coming back with the necessary tools. He uncapped the bottle of lube and squirted a generous amount onto his hand before setting it on the counter and getting close. Calvin pressed his body against my back while gently and thoroughly pushing his fingers into me.

"Like that?" he asked.

I nodded.

"Use your voice," he ordered.

"Yes, I like it."

"You want more?"

"Yes."

Calvin nipped my ear, sucking the lobe as his fingers prodded deep and—*holy shit!*

I cried out and bucked back against his hand.

He laughed quietly and did it again.

"Oh God. Fuck—Cal, please. I-I need it!"

"You *need* it?" he asked, withdrawing his fingers. A brief pause was followed by the crinkle of a condom wrapper and more lube before one hand firmly took my hip.

"You need *any* cock? Or *my* cock, baby?"

"Yours," I said, ignoring the tone of desperation in my voice. I was too worked up to give a damn about being self-conscious now, and maybe Calvin had done that on purpose. "Fuck me—God, before I go insane. No one is as good. I only want you."

I felt his warm breath on the back of my neck, a low laugh escaping as he pressed into me. "Sexy little minx."

I tensed up as Calvin pushed the head of his cock in, and I had to consciously take a few deep breaths. He kissed my neck and shoulder, free hand reaching around to stroke me slowly. He murmured a few words of encouragement while sliding in farther.

"Doing okay?" he asked gently, always ready to break whatever rough play we were having to ensure I was feeling good. And every time, it warmed my heart.

"Okay," I agreed, nodding before pressing my forehead against the wall. "You're really big."

He kissed my head again. "Take your time," Calvin whispered.

I pressed back to meet him after a few more breaths, sliding and locking into place. It felt right and perfect, overwhelming and *good*. "Move."

Calvin pulled back a bit, holding my hips firmly as he slowly thrust in and out. The burning scrape of pleasure sent a thrill from my toes to my head. I moaned in approval and reached down to stroke myself.

Calvin grabbed my hand and pulled it away. "No touching until I say so."

"But I—"

"I'm in charge," he ordered, voice deep and gruff, and fuck—*yes*, God, I'd do anything he said.

"Are you?" I asked, egging him on like he did me. "Then fuck me like you mean it."

Calvin groaned, gripped my hips firm enough to leave marks, and slammed into me. He fucked me with ruthless abandon, balls slapping my ass as he moved hard and fast. I screamed and swore and loved every fucking second of it. Shoved up against the wall, boyfriend's cock buried in my ass, I couldn't comprehend anything but how goddamn perfect the moment was.

"You want me to come in your tight hole?" Calvin

asked.

It was a question I was not meant to disagree with. Not that I wanted to answer to the contrary. "Yes, yes! *Calvin*. Let me come too."

"You hard?" He grunted, and I could barely hear him over the cussing, and moaning, and slapping of skin on skin.

"*Yes*."

Calvin moved one hand from my hip, pulling me back against him so we could manage a kiss. "You're mine. Hear that? You belong to me. Say it."

"I'm yours," I panted. "*Calvin*—!"

"Touch yourself. Come on your hand."

I didn't have to be told twice. I reached down, stroked my cock quickly, and cried out a hell of a lot louder than I intended when I finally was able to come. Calvin gripped me in his arms, shoving in hard a few more times against my tightening muscles before I felt his orgasm rip through his body.

"Holy shit," I swore, wincing as Calvin pulled out. I turned so I could lean back against the wall for support.

Calvin raised my hand, licking my fingers clean.

I smiled weakly when he looked at me after finishing. "Welcome home."

He laughed. "Yeah. One second." Calvin went to the bathroom to toss out the condom.

Legs shaky and uncoordinated as my body still hummed with postsex bliss, I managed to get to the bed and collapse on my back. I tilted my head to watch Calvin walk across the room. He joined me, sliding up against me and putting his head on my chest.

"I'm sorry about what I said."

"Hmm? What did you say that was bad?"

"That you belong to me." Calvin lifted his head to

stare at me. "You're not an object. You don't belong to anyone."

"Oh. Hey, come on, sexy talk in the moment. I know what you mean. You belong to me too, in that 'you're-not-a-possession' kind of way."

Calvin sort of smiled, like he was unsure. "I want to be a good partner for you."

"You are," I said. "You're my knight, remember? What's wrong?"

Calvin put his hand on my chest, rubbing gently. There was a struggle going on, one I could see in his eyes. "I'm not in any position to complain about your ex."

"Neil?"

He looked down, tracing abstract shapes across my skin. "Considering the sort of unorthodox way we ended up together, it seems cruel of me."

"What happened, Calvin?"

"Nothing—very little," he corrected. "Except that he's not over you."

That was a surprise to me. Which maybe was cruel of me as well to think. But after meeting Calvin, it had become apparent to me that I had fallen out of love—at least what I had thought was love—with Neil a long time ago. We had been going through the motions, nothing more.

What happened, happened. I couldn't and wouldn't change the decisions I'd made in December.

I put my hand on Calvin's cheek, caressing his strong features with my thumb. "Did he say something to you?"

"No. He didn't have to say anything."

"I'm sorry. I can't believe he was the forensic guy sent, of all possible people. It didn't turn into some kind of pissing contest, did it? I know I'm all that and a bag of chips, but no need to mark territory."

Calvin snorted. "Funny."

"I'm a bag of expired chips. Stale and kind of funky."

Calvin rolled his eyes. "I kept it in my pants."

"Until you got home. Not complaining. That was fucking amazing." I stroked Calvin's cheek some more, touching my fingertip to individual freckles. "I only mean… I'm sorry I made your job uncomfortable. And I'm sorry that Neil hasn't found closure, but I don't regret choosing you. Not for a minute."

Calvin finally smiled honestly.

"You don't hide me from the world, and that matters. Neil liked having a boyfriend so long as there was no trouble and no drama. Maybe in love with the idea of a boyfriend—not the actual person."

"Did you really feel that way?"

I shrugged a shoulder. "Afterward. Meeting you made me put my love life under a magnifying glass to figure out what the fuck was wrong with it."

Calvin leaned close and kissed me gently. "I love you, Sebastian."

I smiled. "Aw, shucks."

He stared at me for a beat before sitting up. "What's that smell?"

"The sex or the shawarma?"

"Shawarma?" Calvin repeated as he got off the bed. He stretched his arms as he walked to the kitchen counter to investigate the bags.

I dragged my ass off the bed as well, making for the bathroom. "I have to shower. I'm covered in lube."

"Can I join you?"

"Sure. As long as you're not planning to take advantage of me."

I heard Calvin snort as he followed behind me. "Says the man who was just begging for my cock ten minutes ago."

"I wasn't begging."

Calvin shut the door behind us. He got close, slid his arms under my own, and pressed up against my back. "I know you don't like talking during sex. So thank you for that."

I felt the tips of my ears burn and rubbed Calvin's muscular arms briefly. "It's not that I don't like it," I answered. "I just feel lame as hell."

"You were hot," Calvin murmured, kissing the back of my head before letting go. He moved around me and turned the shower on before getting in.

We bumped about, fought over the hot water, and rinsed off the mess of sex. I got dressed after and was watching Calvin put on a pair of jeans and a T-shirt. I didn't see many of those clothes, simply due to the fact the man was *always* working.

Calvin Winter's ass in a pair of jeans was a gift from God.

"Is it my birthday?" I asked, glancing back at him while finally pulling out dinner from the bag.

"Hmm?"

"Nice butt."

Calvin chuckled. "Thanks."

"So," I started, putting the food on two plates. "I've been thinking…."

"Hold on." Calvin went to the fridge and pulled out two beers. He set one down and popped the top off another. He took a swig and then said, "Okay, continue."

"Very funny."

"I thought so."

"I think whoever is behind the notes and the

murders—it's someone I know."

Calvin's expression grew stern, and he leaned back against the counter, crossing his arms. "Go on."

"It's the thing about the bricks in the Emporium. I told you about the cameras?"

"Yes."

"If they had never been in the shop before, they couldn't have sneaked around the cameras so expertly before blacking them out."

Calvin took the plate I handed him. "You believe that?"

"Yeah. I mean, I don't know who it would be—the usual suspects in my life are good people. Plus, there has to be a connection to your cold case, let alone this weird P.T. Barnum stuff going on."

"Seb—"

"What's the story behind Meredith?" I continued, popping open my beer and looking up at Calvin while taking a sip.

He stared. "I'd rather not discuss it now."

"Why?"

"We're eating."

"I can handle it."

Calvin shook his head. "I don't want to bring this kind of negativity home. Not to you."

"That's kind of you, but I'm sort of involved at this point."

"You don't know how to take a hint, do you?" Calvin asked, but he had a funny little smile on his face. Not entirely amused, but not wholly annoyed either.

"If I did, I wouldn't have gotten you," I tried, wiggling my eyebrows. "Come on, Detective. Humor me."

Calvin leaned against the counter and took a big

bite of his dinner. I pulled up a nearby barstool and sat, waiting with as much patience as someone like me has, watching Calvin inhale his food, per usual.

"Meredith's daughter was found dead in her bedroom by her boyfriend, who called 911. The girl's bag had been packed and the boyfriend said she was planning to move out after too many fights with her mother. The girl's skull had been broken in several places—medical examiner ruled the weapon was likely a hammer."

"Let me guess. No hammer was found?"

Calvin nodded. "Meredith owned a complete and well-used toolkit, with the hammer missing. She claimed to not know where it had vanished."

"What about her alibi?"

"She had been working. Her boss agreed."

"Why was it not believed?"

"Because no one remembered seeing her the night of the murder," Calvin said. "The bouncer said she never worked Tuesdays. The other dancers were shady, to say the least."

"Afraid to speak up?"

"Likely."

"Was there any surveillance pulled from the club?"

Calvin shook his head. "It was a shithole. No recording and backing up to drives or online storage. And the physical tape, the boss recorded over."

"Convenient."

"Yeah."

"Did the investigation end there?"

Calvin nodded again. "No one would come forward, we couldn't find the murder weapon, and the only DNA we found was mishandled by a rookie with CSU who forgot how to do their job." He popped the last piece of food in his mouth and turned to set the plate in the sink.

"Anyway," he said around chewing. "The crime got a lot of press until the Harrison case." He turned to me. "Do you remember that?"

"That was the nutcase who murdered his family in their penthouse apartment and tossed the bodies off the balcony. I guess people would stop caring about a poor, nobody girl after that."

"New York," Calvin muttered, shaking his head.

"Hey," I said, prodding him in the side. "We're not all crazy."

"You're a little crazy, sweetie. But I think it's in the water."

"Then you're crazy too."

"You've been drinking the water longer."

"Let's see," I said, resting my plate on my lap so I could do some math on my fingers. "When did you move to New York—after college?"

Calvin nodded. "To apply to the police academy."

"Twenty-one?"

"Yes."

"I was... oh God, I was only twelve?" Calvin made a face, and I started laughing. "You cradle-robber."

When I woke up the next morning, I was alone. I groaned into my pillow and rolled over more, grabbing Calvin's and pressing it against my face. It smelled like him, but it was cool to the touch. Cracking an eye open, I looked toward the window to see brightness behind the closed blinds.

I couldn't remember the last time I'd woken up without an alarm. Even on my one day off a week, I always got up early. Between owning a business and having bills and an assistant to pay, I had family obligations, boyfriend duties, and shitty errands, like, you know, grocery shopping on occasion. I never slept late.

"Ten o'clock?" I asked myself in disbelief after putting on my glasses and checking my phone. I also had five text messages. God, had I slept through a tornado and aliens landing in Central Park too?

One from Max. *Hey, boss, did your landlord call you?*

One from Pop. *Good morning, kiddo. Give me a call today. Love you.*

One from Beth. *Max visited and told me what happened! If you need anything, call me!*

Two from Calvin. *Don't do anything today that involves me finding you at a murder scene.*

And lastly: *You drooled on me last night. Buy me a beer at O'Neil's Pub and I won't tell anyone.*

Damn it. I'd been awake for thirty seconds and already I was being threatened and blackmailed.

I chose Max as the best person to respond to first and typed a message while climbing out of bed. *No. Ehy?*

I walked over to the kitchenette and started a pot of coffee. My phone dinged as the heavenly beverage was bubbling, breaking the quiet of Calvin's tiny studio. I picked it up, bringing it close to read.

I bumped into him outside the Emporium. He's kind of a jerk for real.

I snorted. To say the least. Luther was an okay landlord, so long as I never needed anything and paid my rent the first of the month, preferably first thing in the morning or I'd start getting reminder texts. That and his snide, I'm-not-judging-your-gayness-but-I-really-totally-am comments now and then. I typically ignored them. I wasn't going to waste my breath arguing with someone like Luther. But maybe the next time he had some "but I never understand which one is the *woman*," comment, I'd let him direct that at Calvin and see how well it goes over.

Ignore iit. I wll call hum.

I set the phone aside, poured cream into a mug, and filled it with fresh coffee. I wished Calvin had woken me before he left, but it was typical of him. Maybe it was because he had dated so little before meeting me that it was simply something he wasn't used to—or perhaps he didn't realize I wanted to say good-bye? But then again, I liked the way we worked. I know some don't get it, but I don't enjoy mushy declarations of love at every corner. Stretching them out into little intimate moments was much more pleasing, and Calvin functioned on the same wavelength.

Except… Valentine's Day. I think I really did want to try having one super romantic date, with flowers and holding hands and kissing and all the corny stuff. And if I grew a pair and told Calvin to go out with me in a few days, I knew he would, but would he be as into it as me?

I wanted him to genuinely enjoy it, and I wasn't so sure he would. But I had more important things to mull over while drinking my first cup of the morning.

Like murder.

I hummed quietly. Calvin had given me a little to work with last night. There didn't seem to be a reason to suspect the boyfriend who found Meredith's daughter, and the unanimous yet unspoken agreement appeared to be that Meredith's boss knew and was covering for her. The physical evidence that would likely be the case-breaker was the missing hammer. But it could be anywhere. A dumpster, the Hudson River—fucking Staten Island, for all I and anyone else knew.

But I wondered if it wasn't that complex. It didn't sound premeditated. A hammer was intimate, brutal, and like a crime of sudden and uncontrollable rage. What if Meredith panicked and hid the hammer? What if she didn't know how to dispose of it?

And her boss—Ricky, I was assuming. Why would she go out of her way to tell him? Maybe they had been an item. Or maybe she knew he could help… what… hide the weapon? From what Calvin had told me last night, the mess-up with DNA evidence had hurt his case. Had he never gotten legal warrants to search Ricky's club?

That would explain why the case went cold.

I took a big gulp of the remaining coffee. "But I'm not a cop."

And I don't need a warrant.

CHAPTER EIGHT

"You want me to what?" Max asked, his voice on loudspeaker and the phone on the bed as I moved around the apartment, getting dressed.

"Look someone up on Facebook."

"Who am I Face-stalking and why?"

"His name is Roger Trim," I called before pulling on yesterday's T-shirt. "And you're not stalking."

"Sorta, yeah, I am. Tell me why."

"Because I don't know how."

"You're the best-looking ninety-year-old man I know," Max replied. "I mean, why are you curious?"

"I'm a cat—I can't resist."

"You're full of it this morning."

I sat on the bed to put my shoes on. Roger Trim was the name of the boyfriend. Specifically, Wendy Brown's— the deceased daughter of the more recently deceased Meredith Brown, so said the articles I'd checked that morning. "I want to know where he works. People put that on Facebook, don't they?"

"Sometimes. But he might not even have a public account."

"Are you checking?"

"You're so pushy. Hold on," Max grumbled. "Who is this guy? You swinging now?"

"What? *No*," I said forcefully while looking down at the phone. "I am not. Thank you."

"Good. You're way too monogamous to enjoy playing around," Max replied, and I could hear the clicking of computer keys just under his voice.

"Don't say that like it's a bad thing."

"I'm not. I mean, you know, you're so domestic and cute and shit with Calvin."

"Domestic and cute and shit?" I repeated slowly.

"Yeah. When's the wedding?"

"Hilarious."

"I'm assuming I'm hunting for Roger Trims in New York City?"

"Yup."

"Whoa. Uh, how old is this dude?"

"I don't know—maybe around twenty by now?"

"Oh, okay."

"Why?" I asked, standing once more and grabbing my sweater.

"Silver fox."

I rolled my eyes and didn't bother replying. I tugged on a sort of threadbare and frumpy-looking thing, buttoned it, and patted my magnifying glass in the front pocket. After Max had been quiet for another minute, I asked, "So?"

"There are a few Roger Trims. Do you know what he looks like?"

"Nope."

"Helpful. I'll just go with the younger guys." He sighed. "So one of the Rogers lists his hometown as Brooklyn, twenty-eight, and works at Taylor & Taylor International Tax Firm."

I frowned, slowly shaking my head as I returned to the phone on the bed. "I don't think so. I get the impression he's not a six-figure-a-year sort of guy."

"Hold on—here's the other. Says he's twenty-one and works at Tall, Dark, and Bitter."

"Is that a joke?"

"No, it's a coffee shop."

"It is?"

"Yeah, in Midtown on the East Side. You've never been there?"

"Apparently not."

"It's a nice place. They have a cake called Murdered by German Chocolate."

They did have the murder cake.

In fact, Tall, Dark, and Bitter seemed to get a kick out of menu names and didn't miss a beat from beverage to dessert. The café was up on Twenty-Eighth Street, squished between a yogurt shop and a bank. It was dim inside, with dark-colored walls and tables, and those funky, paper-looking light fixtures from IKEA. There were couches and coffee tables near the back, and a long bar and register to the right as I walked in. A big, fancy chalkboard hung behind, decked out with their colorfully worded menu.

Most of the tables were full with early lunch-goers, so I took a seat at the bar. I had to squint hard to read the menu from that far away. Jumpstart the Ticker Espresso,

Double Shot Heart Attack, Murder She Latte—I was hesitant to drink the coffee here.

"Howdy," a young guy said as he slid into view in front of me. "Help you?"

"Uh, I guess," I said, looking at him. Was this Roger Trim? He was young enough, but there were several employees mingling about. "I think I'll stay away from those coffees and get some lunch."

"I suggest the Flat on the Freeway Burger."

I nodded. "Do I need a tetanus shot first?"

He smiled. "It's just a turkey burger. But it's really good."

"Sure."

"Want Brains with that?" He leaned over the counter. "Curly fries with ketchup," he whispered.

"Ah. Why not. Dead freeway bird and brains, please."

He chuckled and wrote the order on a menu pad. "I'll be back with it soon."

I pulled out my cell as he walked through a door that must have led to the kitchen. I picked Max from my contacts and gave him a call.

"Yo, Sleuthy McSleutherson."

"No, it's Sebastian."

"I think I have Sleuthy on the phone," Max answered.

I sighed. "Can you send me a picture of the guy?"

"If by doing so, are you going to do something illegal, and does that make me an accomplice?"

"No."

"Why do I not believe you," Max said absently.

"What do you want in return?"

"A raise."

"Fat chance. I'm homeless. If either of us is getting

a raise, it's me."

"I'll take some of TDB's cake, then."

"Done."

"All right, I'll send you a text. Just don't creep on the guy." Max hung up.

My phone vibrated a minute later and a picture loaded. Yup, same guy, except his Facebook profile picture was of him with two straws in his mouth—walrus imitation, I guess. Now I was here, found the guy, and just needed to get a conversation going about his dead girlfriend.

Sure. That'd go over well.

I pushed up my old sunglasses and typed into the internet browser. Sure enough, I found Meredith Brown's murder mentioned in the news headlines. None too classy either. *Suspect Stripper Served Justice! Murderous Mommy Found Dead!*

I bet Calvin was thrilled about those.

Roger came out of the kitchen a few minutes later with a big plate and set it down in front of me. "Here you are."

I glanced up and took the only chance I saw. "Have you seen the news today? This exotic dancer they found dead at the history museum? It said she was a suspect two years ago when her daughter was murdered." Even with my less-than-stellar vision, I could see Roger's expression slide right off his face. He looked a little sick.

"Really? Who was she?"

I feigned ignorance and looked at the phone again. "Meredith Brown."

"Holy shit."

I looked up. "Did you know her?"

"That bitch—" He immediately clamped a hand over his mouth and glanced at the patrons nearby. "No, it's nothing. I, uh, sorry."

"It's okay," I insisted. "You should sit down, though."

"I'm fine," he said defensively, but he looked like he was having trouble holding it together. "Does it… say how she died?"

"Er…." I glanced at the article. It did not, and Calvin probably wouldn't appreciate that information being leaked by moi. "No, sorry. Were you acquaintances?"

Roger looked up and snorted loudly. "As if. She was… was… my girlfriend's mom. She killed my girlfriend," he whispered, and now I felt like shit because his eyes were starting to well up.

I grabbed my napkin and handed it to him, then watched Roger wipe his face. "Oh. I'm sorry," I said quietly. "I really am."

"It's fine, man. You didn't know." He tossed out the napkin and handed me a new one from a container. "But I won't pretend to be sad she's gone. She treated Wendy like shit. And finally Wendy had had enough, and she was going to move in with me, and we were going to go to school together up in Vermont. We had it all planned out."

I nodded. "Why didn't the police arrest her?"

"I don't know. I told them she killed Wendy. With a *hammer*, dude," he said, sounding very much like a kid again as he spilled his guts to me. "I can't… even think about it that much without wanting to barf. I told the police they had been fighting, that her mom was a piece of shit. She was dating the sleazy creep who owns the strip club she danced at."

"But how did you know it was the mom?" I tried gently, keeping my voice low.

Roger frowned and leaned on the bar top. "I mean, I wasn't there to see it, but it couldn't have been anyone else. She hated Wendy. Resented having a kid. Everyone knew it too. My girlfriend was amazing. She was so smart. She was going to be a lawyer. Can you believe that?" He picked up a rag from under the counter and scrubbed vigorously at a stain that wasn't there. "You won't see me shedding a tear for her mom."

"Whatever happened to the hammer?"

Roger shrugged. "I always thought Meredith gave it to Ricky."

I felt myself lean closer. "Why?"

"I spent more time in the same room with that ass-clown than I ever wanted. He always used to brag about the safe he kept in a little room somewhere behind the dancers' dressing room. Ricky was always saying that if cops ever came after him, they'd never find anything. Whatever *anything* was supposed to mean.... Meredith had him agree to her bogus story, so I figured she ran to him after, he hid the hammer in his safe, and it hasn't been seen since."

The door to Ricky's was locked. And it had started raining again.

I moved to a nearby doorway, standing under the little awning and watching my target. No one came or left. I guess lap dances weren't popular at just after one on a workday. The sky cracked and roared, and a bright flash of lightning tore in between skyscrapers. The rain came in a sudden torrent, rushing down the streets and into drains, washing out the sidewalk, and causing other pedestrians to make mad dashes for awnings like I had.

"Jesus," I swore, stuffing my hands into my pockets and suppressing a shiver as the wind picked up.

What am I doing?

Being a busybody, that's what I was doing. I wasn't

somewhere safe, like I should have been. I wasn't listening to Calvin, and I hadn't learned my lesson. I wanted to see this through to the possibly bitter end.

I wanted to prove Meredith Brown killed her daughter, just like the note told me to do. Because I wanted to know what would happen next. I wanted it to bring me closer to who had blown up my home and killed people. And I wanted to understand the Barnum connection when there appeared to be no rhyme or reason.

So I stood there scowling and waiting.

The violence of the sudden storm eased over the course of about thirty minutes, but it was still coming down at a steady and freezing rate when a big delivery van came to a stop, double-parking outside of Ricky's. A guy jumped out of the passenger seat and moved around the back to hoist up the door. From my view it looked like furniture inside, and I suspected some sort of party rental shop. A second man came around the back from the driver's side, and they both started pulling carefully packed items from the van.

The door to Ricky's swung open next, and a guy stepped out briefly to shout something I couldn't make out, motion with his hands, and then prop the door open for the movers. He vanished back inside afterward. I perked up, watching for someone else to come out or something to happen, but the door just stood open, and despite the rain, the movers took their sweetass time.

I stepped out from under the awning, hunching my shoulders as rain found its way down the back of my collar. I walked by the front door, glancing inside. It was dim and hard to make much out, but no one stood there to block me from entering.

"Should have had this shit delivered on pallets," one mover griped. "Cheap fuck."

"I'm too old to be breaking my back like this," the

other said.

All right, so they weren't paying any attention. I looked back at the door and took a step inside before I could think too much about the consequences.

The club's lights were low. The place was bedazzled with Valentine's Day decorations, which was a little strange if you asked me. Loads of gaudy paper hearts and cupids hung from the ceiling. The tables had fake candles and what looked like plastic rose petals thrown across them.

How romantic.

I hastily walked through the throng of smaller tables and past the main stage. A stairwell near the back led upstairs, but once I got close, the sign indicated Private Parties. Not what I wanted. Definitely not. I found another door, though, and that said Employees Only, so I walked right in.

I entered a short hall with three more doors. The first stood ajar and I peeked inside, but it was only a supply closet. The door right beside it was closed, and I could hear a muffled, one-sided conversation. My gut told me it was the same man who'd gone out to greet the movers, since I hadn't seen any other employees yet.

Maybe he was *The* Ricky?

I moved to the right side of the hall and glanced into the last open door. It was a fairly large dressing room, dark except for one of those makeup mirrors turned on near the back. It cast a weird, sort of uncomfortable glow in the room, and if I hadn't heard the office door opening behind me, I might not have gone inside.

"Yeah, I'll give you a call back," Suspect-Ricky said as he walked into the hall.

I dove into the dressing room, bumping into chairs and getting tangled in a robe left on the floor. I looked behind me to see his shape silhouetted against the brightness of the hallway.

"Yesterday," he said. "Meredith was my best goddamn dancer. No. Split her bookings between Abby and Jess. They should be able to handle it."

The show must go on, I guess.

"Look, I've got guys moving shit in here for the V-Day shindig. I need to go pay them. All right, yeah, bye."

I stumbled farther into the room and ducked behind a rack of clothes when Ricky turned in my direction. I held my breath, peeking behind a few garments to see him enter and make his way directly toward me.

Oh *fuck*.

Don't look this way, don't look this way, I silently chanted.

Ricky walked right by the clothing rack and went to the wall. I moved aside a few clothes to peek out and see what he was doing. Ricky pushed aside a table and hoisted a big potted plant out of the way. He crouched down near the floor and lifted something. Suddenly a small portion of the wall swung open.

Hidden door?

I perked up.

I could hear Ricky moving about inside. Getting in once he left seemed easy enough, but the problem was the safe. How could I get the evidence without getting caught and then having it dismissed by a court because I was an asshole? Lying would only make it worse, but I was seriously considering some not-totally-outrageous storylines as to how I could have found the hammer—if it were there at all.

I fumbled my phone free from my pocket and pulled up a text message. I never thought this recently learned tool would be handy, but I sent Calvin a map of my current location. He'd warned not to find me at a murder scene, and if one were being technical, I wasn't at one.

Calvin's name immediately popped up on the screen, phone buzzing in my hand. I canceled the call and put it back in my pocket. Sorry, honey, not now.

A woman entered the room just then, crying. She dropped her bag and coat on a chair and wiped her face while walking to the secret room. "Ricky!" She sounded like the same young lady who answered my call the day before.

"*What*?" Ricky snapped from inside the room. "I'm busy."

"Ricky, I just read in the papers. Meredith, she's—she's—"

"I know, baby," he called.

I frowned. Baby was *my* pet name, thank you very much, sir.

The girl stood in the open doorway to the room. "Aren't you going to do anything?" she protested.

"What the fuck do you expect me to do? She's dead," Ricky barked.

Damn. What an asshole.

The girl sniffed and gingerly wiped under her eyes. "I knew it. I knew she shouldn't have left with that guy. He must have… oh my God, poor Mere!"

"What guy?" Ricky asked, and I'm glad he did, because I almost jumped out of the clothing rack and asked myself.

She glanced up, staring at Ricky, who was still hidden from view inside the room. "T-there was a guy on Wednesday afternoon who picked her up when we were having a smoke outside."

"Who was this guy, Gracie?" Ricky asked, sounding more and more pissed by the second.

"I don't know. I don't think Meredith knew him."

"But?"

"But, I mean, she got in the truck with him. I don't know why. Poor Mere!" Gracie started sobbing again.

"You fucking *bitch*," Ricky shouted. "You saw the guy and didn't tell anyone? Meredith was my prize!"

"I-I'm sorry! I didn't realize something was wrong."

Inside the room, I heard Ricky drop something and then metal grate against metal. The first thing I thought was "He has a gun in his safe."

"Ricky?" Gracie asked, her tone hesitant and decidedly scared. She took a step back from the doorway.

And then Ricky lunged out of the room, wielding a hammer and swinging at the girl's face. She screamed and stumbled back, tripping over her own feet and falling to the floor. She curled into a ball, trying in vain to protect herself.

I didn't have a second to think. A second would have been too long. I dove out from the clothing rack and tackled Ricky from the side, throwing him to the floor and away from Gracie. He swore and swung the hammer, which was still in his grip. I struggled against him, trying to get his arms under control.

"Get out!" I shouted at Gracie, not bothering to look and see if she was already gone. "*Run.*"

I heard her cry and gasp and then the clicking of her heels pounded the floor as she escaped.

"Get the fuck off me," Ricky snarled, and he got his foot on my chest and shoved hard.

I flew backward and landed on the floor. Ricky appeared over me with the hammer. He reached down, grabbed the front of my jacket in one hand, and lifted me toward him. I fought and tried to shove him, but he had a better position and I couldn't reach his arm when he pulled the hammer back.

Man… I was one shitty warrior. Save the girl, get bludgeoned for my efforts.

Ricky brought the hammer down. I struggled and fought violently, managing to miss being smashed over the head. Instead he got me in the side. It was enough to make me gasp and lose my hold on him. I fought to catch my breath, and Ricky raised the hammer again.

A deafening shot pierced the room.

My ears rang.

Ricky stumbled, dropped the hammer, and crashed to the floor. My breath was heavy sounding, muted, and weird. I collapsed onto my back and tilted my head to look at the door upside down.

Calvin lowered his SIG P226.

CHAPTER NINE

"I was supposed to buy Max some death cake."

"What?"

"Murder cake, I mean."

Calvin let out a long sigh.

I was sitting at one of the tables in the front of Ricky's club. There were police everywhere, and paramedics were bringing him out on a stretcher from the back hall. The fuck was damn lucky Calvin was a good cop and had given him a not-too-serious wound. I turned to watch Ricky get wheeled by.

He flipped me the finger.

I raised my hand to shoot the gesture right back at him, but Calvin put his hand firmly over my own, stopping me.

"Sebastian. I can't decide if you're purposefully trying to get yourself killed, or if you're only trying to put me in an early grave."

"You caught me. Am I in your will so I benefit

from your riches?"

Calvin pushed his coat open to rest his hands on his hips. "Yes. You get my dirty laundry and PlayStation."

"Score."

"What the hell are you doing here?" he asked next, staring down at me.

"Sleuthing."

"No shit."

"I found the hammer," I pointed out. "Meredith must have given it to Ricky after she killed her daughter. He kept it in a safe. Do you think there are still fingerprints or DNA?"

Calvin clenched his jaw, but after a moment of mental counting to ensure he didn't strangle his idiot boyfriend, he said, "There's old blood and fingerprints on it. It'll match Meredith and her daughter, Wendy, no doubt."

I nodded. "So… case closed."

"Why did you come here?" Calvin asked again.

"I talked to the old boyfriend," I said, looking up. "He's the one who knew about the safe." I offered Calvin an awkward smile. "Want me to tell a convincing story? I came by to ask about their Valentine's Day show. I got lost looking for an employee, walked in on Ricky getting ready to beat the shit out of that girl—" I pointed over toward Gracie, who was being questioned by Quinn. "And then… you know."

"Real believable."

"Is it because I'm gay?"

"Don't be cute."

"We can say I was inquiring for Max. He'd probably like a lap dance."

"How did you find Roger?" Calvin asked. "The boyfriend?"

"Don't you remember me telling you everything can be found online these days? Max calls it Face-stalking."

Calvin didn't look any happier. His jaw was clenched again, and the muscles in his neck tensed. I realized the expression was stress. A lot of it.

"Cal?" I asked. "Are you okay?"

He didn't answer.

Quinn strode across the room and nodded at Calvin as she reached us. "Gracie Madison works here. Answers phones, fills in dancing when one of the other girls calls out. She says Ricky attacked her and she doesn't know where Mr. White Knight came from, only that he saved her from being beaten with a hammer."

I nodded and looked back at Calvin. "I did do that. That part is true."

Quinn looked down at me and raised an eyebrow. "Anyway. Cupcake over there said she saw Meredith Brown get into a truck with a guy on Wednesday, about an hour or so before she was murdered at the museum."

Calvin immediately moved to go speak with Gracie. When I stood up, he put a firm hand on my shoulder and pushed me back into the seat. "Not you. Stay."

"I'm not a dog."

"Dogs take better direction." He left me and walked to her table.

"Aren't you two precious," Quinn said.

I frowned and turned toward the other table. Calvin towered over Gracie, looking down at her as she spoke with her hands. She was still scared and nervous and was talking fast, but I was able to pick up parts of her side of the conversation.

"A big guy. Fat."

"No. No, I don't think so."

"Like construction, I guess."

"Well… no, but I noticed on the truck it said North. North *something*."

"Calvin. Wait, listen," I insisted, grabbing his jacket sleeve and holding him back.

The police closed Ricky's for what I imagined was the foreseeable future and were wrapping the scene up as Calvin made to leave.

"I'm driving you to your father's," Calvin answered.

"*Wait*," I said again, more firmly. "For Christ's sake."

Calvin frowned and looked down at me. "Sebastian. I'm pissed. I can't believe you—"

"I know who Gracie saw," I whispered harshly.

"You have my undivided attention," Quinn butted in. She lightly smacked Calvin's chest when he began to protest.

"I'm certain whoever is behind this is someone who knows me. It has to be. It's been so personal. But she claims to have seen a big guy driving a construction truck that had North on the side?" I couldn't believe I was going to say this. "The Emporium's landlord. Luther North. He owns a small construction company called North's Buildings and Repairs. And yes, he's a rather overweight gent."

No matter how sly you can be, the silliest mistake will always be your undoing. Luther drove the damn truck advertising his name for the world to see. He picked Meredith up, brought her to the museum, and killed her. He had access to my shop, he knew where I lived….

"*And* I proved the case," I said to Calvin. "I'm owed a mermaid."

Calvin's face was hard. "Where do you think it'll show?" he finally asked.

I shrugged. "The Emporium is where it all began with the bricks. It's as good a place as any."

Quinn looked up at Calvin. "Want to go fishing?"

Calvin let out a held breath and ran a hand through his hair. "When writing my obituary, just be sure it says, 'Sebastian was the death of him.'" He turned and walked to the exit.

"Ha, ha," I said loudly, following. "Heart disease is more believable."

Calvin turned as he held the door open for Quinn and I. "Not once people meet you, Seb."

I stood in the doorway, looking up at him. "Look—"

Calvin shook his head. "Not now."

No arguing with that, then.

I walked outside into a mix of rain and snow—cold and miserable. The sun was already setting and I startled, realizing I'd been inside the grubby club for several hours. Where was hand sanitizer when I needed it?

I headed toward Calvin's car, then paused when a uniformed officer tipped her cap at me.

"Evening, Mr. Snow."

It was Brigg, the poor responding officer to all of my out-of-this-world calls at the Emporium. "Hi," I said in passing.

Quinn opened the door to the backseat of Calvin's car and got inside. She looked at me as I approached. "You can have the front."

"He doesn't like me at the moment."

"Poor baby." She shut the door.

Damn it.

I opened the passenger door and climbed in.

Calvin followed, started the car, and swiftly merged into traffic. He took a left at the end of the block, heading downtown on Ninth Avenue. Evening rush hour was already starting. Bicyclists neglected the bike lane and wove through cars, pedestrians crossed when and where they pleased, and cabs seemed to be giving it their best effort to ignore lights and signs.

Calvin handled it all like a native New Yorker.

"Who taught you how to drive?"

He looked sideways briefly. "Why?"

I shrugged.

He was quiet for a beat. "My big brother."

"What's his name?"

It had never come up. Calvin *never* spoke about his family. Not even in passing. I only knew what that photo under his bed had told me—parents and two siblings. Hell, I'd only known whatever relationship he had with them soured completely when Calvin decided to come out in order to make us work. His father calling yesterday was the first bit of communication I'd been privy to, and what had I gleaned from it?

Retired military.

Asshole.

And that was about it. I didn't even know his father's name. So the fact that Calvin had uttered a word about his older brother had me on the edge of my seat for more information.

I watched Calvin look into the rearview mirror a few times. Possibly at traffic; more likely at Quinn. Did she know about his family? They had been working together months before I came into the picture. I supposed it was possible, considering the extensive time they spent with each other.

"Marc."

"What?"

Calvin looked at me briefly. "His name is Marc."

I twisted my fingers together, trying to keep conversation casual. Sometimes Calvin made learning more about him harder than pulling teeth. I knew he had reasons for not talking about himself. I did. I only wished he would understand that it was important to me to know because I cared about him. I was supposed to know these things about Calvin. Like it or not. That was basically rule number one in the boyfriend hand guide, right?

"What's he do?"

Calvin didn't answer right away. He was quiet for several blocks, and I thought that had been it.

"He's an architect."

Well, then. All I needed now was to know his blood type, and I'd have learned all there was regarding Marc Winter, the architect.

"What about your sister?"

"Not now, Sebastian."

Shot down.

I looked into the passenger mirror and caught Quinn's gaze. She didn't seem surprised by the mention of Calvin's brother. Part of me hoped she didn't know more than I did, but then I considered, if she did, that meant Calvin was talking to *someone.* And he needed that. He desperately needed to talk, because he kept everything inside, and I was afraid of how he would try coping when it all finally boiled over.

It was slow progress getting across town to the East Village, but at least it had stopped spitting snow and rain by the time Calvin found a place to park on the Emporium's block. We all climbed out of the car. I rubbed my side where Ricky had grazed me with the hammer. I'd really been lucky.

"Max isn't at the shop today, is he?" Calvin asked as he rounded the front of the car and stood at my side. He put a hand on my shoulder and held me back from taking a step toward the Emporium.

I made a face and looked up at him. "No, why?"

"There's a light on."

"*What*?" I turned back to the storefront. Just through the metal gate and newly replaced window, I could see a faint illumination. My office light, maybe? "Oh hell no," I said, trying to walk to the door again.

"Stay back," Calvin ordered firmly. He pulled me out of view of the window, standing off to the side. "Quinn, there's an alley in between."

I hastily reached into my pockets, pulled out keys, and moved to the alley door between mine and Beth's shops. I unlocked it and tugged it open. Quinn pulled her weapon and nodded at Calvin before vanishing down the walkway.

"Sebastian."

I turned around.

"Open the gate."

I went back to the front door and did as I was told, quickly getting the gate lifted, which anyone inside would hear. By anyone, I meant Luther North. Because it had to be him. Which really pissed me off, because I was a good tenant and never complained, until my window was busted, at least…. I mean, what the fuck was his problem? I knew he was a bit of a homophobic dickhead, but this had nothing to do with my preferred bedroom partner.

He was stalking me. Killing people. All in the name of curiosity. No one had run out the back door yet, because surely we'd have heard Quinn. So he—Luther—was still inside. Doing what, though? Hiding? Hoping I had come by for normal work and not specifically because we'd cracked the case of Meredith Brown and Calvin was going to arrest his sweaty ass?

Maybe I had left the light on Wednesday evening. It was hard to remember. It felt like ages ago.

"Give me your keys," Calvin said.

"No."

"Don't argue," he said firmly, holding one hand out and pulling his gun with the other.

I glanced at people walking by, who saw the gun and immediately moved away from Calvin. Not that he gave off bad-guy vibes, but he wasn't in uniform and didn't drive a cruiser, so I didn't blame folks.

I handed over the set of keys.

"Stay here," he said sternly before approaching the front door.

Sure I would.

Calvin unlocked the door to the Emporium, pushed it open, and slipped inside. I grabbed it before it could shut behind him, and poked my head in. I watched Calvin's back as he moved through the dim shop toward the light in the back.

Still.

Silent.

Nothing.

And then….

"Freeze!" Calvin shouted, his body stance changing as he pointed his gun. "Hands where I can see them."

Holy motherfucking shit, someone was really in my shop. World, I seemed to have gotten on a roller-coaster ride back in December. May my boyfriend and I get off? I'm much more of a teacup person.

I stepped inside when I saw Quinn walk through the shadows from the back, weapon trained on a target I couldn't see around Calvin. She holstered her SIG before taking a pair of handcuffs from her coat. I heard her snap the cuffs on and give the guy his rights. She then asked if he had anything in his pockets that could hurt her while she searched him. Calvin didn't move a muscle as he waited for Quinn to finish.

"Is it him?" I asked, not that Calvin had ever met Luther before.

Calvin didn't take his eyes off his target. "Just once would it kill you to listen to me?"

Maybe not, but why take the chance?

I walked down the first narrow aisle, coming up behind Calvin. I moved to his right, looking around him. "I fucking knew it."

Luther was standing by my counter, hands behind his back. I slipped by Calvin as he lowered his weapon, and could see the wild, terrified look on Luther's face. Yeah, I guess having a gun aimed at your head would scare the shit out of anyone.

"Sebastian," he said, sounding awfully surprised. "What're you doing here?"

"It's my store. Should I have called first to make sure you weren't breaking and entering?"

"*Sebastian*," Calvin said firmly.

Quinn directed Luther toward the steps and made him sit down.

The middle step creaked under his full weight.

I glanced over my shoulder to see Calvin with his phone to his ear before I joined Luther. "Why'd you do it?" I asked, suddenly feeling exhausted as the epic conclusion turned out to not be so epic. "I was almost blown up. Some nutcase tried to kill me with a hammer."

"Huh?" Luther's face was blotchy, the varying gray tones making it look like he was going to be sick or maybe have a heart attack.

"My apartment."

"What about it?"

I looked at Calvin again. He was watching Luther while talking to someone on the other end of the call. I crouched down to be eye level with Luther. "You started this whole mess, didn't you? The bricks? The—"

"No, I didn't do that. I… I knew about it, but it wasn't me."

"Then how did they get inside, if it wasn't you?"

"I don't know."

"Luther!"

"*I don't know*!" he shouted at me. "He told me if I didn't follow directions, he'd throw me in jail."

I looked up when Quinn took a step forward, but she didn't speak. Instead she nodded at me to continue. I could say whatever I wanted to Luther. I wasn't a cop. If he freely talked to me and two detectives overheard it all, versus him clamming up and demanding a lawyer when they asked….

"Who told you?"

Luther shook his head and looked down. "A cop," he muttered. "He said he was a cop, anyway."

"A cop threatened you to threaten me?"

Luther shrugged his big shoulders and then nodded.

"Who was he?"

"He didn't tell me his fucking name," Luther shouted, staring back at me. "You dumb son of a—"

"*Hey*," Calvin said, shutting Luther the hell up. "Watch it."

Luther's face was starting to sweat. "I saw him once. I swear. Then I only got text messages."

"Telling you what to do?"

"Yeah. But it wasn't—I never did anything illegal."

"You broke into my store just now," I pointed out. "How's that not illegal?"

"I'm the landlord."

"You still need to ask me."

"Fuck you, Sebastian. God, you are such an arrogant little queer!"

Calvin moved beside me, using his towering height and build to put the fear of God into Luther. "One more word about him," he said in a calm, calculating tone, "and you and I are going to have a problem."

Luther swallowed compulsively, and I feared he'd choke on his tongue. He looked back at me, away from Calvin's terrifying glare. "He only told me to drop something off here."

"And?" I prodded.

"And—and I was supposed to pick up some chick on Wednesday."

"You killed her."

"I didn't kill anyone," Luther argued. "I picked up some fucking stripper and brought her to the damn history museum. My text message said to bring her to the whale exhibit and then leave. That's all I did! She's not—is she dead?"

"Yeah," I answered. "Someone shot her in the chest."

Luther moved instinctively to grab a tissue from his pocket, but his hands cuffed behind his back halted the motion. He tried to wipe his face on his shoulder, which was just awkward. "I didn't. I swear. I just didn't want to go to jail."

I shook my head. What an *idiot*. "Who was the cop?"

"I told you I don't—"

"What did he look like?" I pressured.

"Like, I don't know. No one special. A guy."

"Luther!"

"He was just a guy!" Luther shouted. "Kind of tall, but not that big. And about your age, you shit."

I ignored the comment, because really, what was the point of fighting a jerk who was already in handcuffs? "What was his hair color?"

"Pink."

I recoiled in confusion. "What?"

"Blue. *Purple*. What the hell does it matter to you? It's all *gray*, right?"

"All right," Calvin said, forcefully but gently pushing me aside. "Stand up." He grabbed Luther by one arm and the handcuffs, hoisted the big guy to his feet, and walked him away. "That's enough."

I stood as the front door opened, uniformed officers stepping inside and heading directly toward Calvin and Luther.

It *was* all gray.

I can't say why that hurt so deeply, because I was a kid once and lived through years of teasing because of my condition, but that one snide comment made me feel... useless. If I can't tell the difference between blue and pink, how could I possibly do any complex task? And it's not like I couldn't see them as two distinct colors. Blue and pink are two different shades.

But still gray.

Everything was always gray in the end.

Luther's fat, sweaty face was gray.

Calvin's beautiful eyes were gray.

My entire world, for all its monochromatic beauty, was missing something essential. And I couldn't even properly describe the absence of color because I never knew it was a concept to begin with. Like missing a friend I never met.

"You okay?" Quinn nudged my arm. "I've got to go

talk with Calvin."

I quickly nodded and pushed my sunglasses up, lest she see I was getting emotional about what most people consider nothing. "Sure. Go ahead."

She waited a moment because she knew I wasn't okay, but Quinn had priorities, and my feelings were not at the top of that list.

I went up the steps and walked by the counter with the brass register, making for my office. The light was on inside, and sitting on my desk was a gross, dried-out animal corpse.

The mermaid.

Although technically it was a blackened and leathered monkey, with the lower half cut away and replaced with a fish tail. The animal looked to have died in agony, and after a hundred and fifty plus years, it had not aged well. I pulled out my magnifying glass and took a look, guessing that the missing hair was due to moths or rodents or poor storage. Likewise, the scales of the fish tail were basically gone. But this couldn't be mistaken for anything else. It looked exactly like the drawings from Barnum's time.

Hideous.

There was a folded note beside the mermaid. I picked it up and read it.

Congratulations!

Gee, thanks.

But there's more.

That sounded like a shitty infomercial.

I unfolded the rest of the note.

Visitors needed a guide to Thebes. Tomorrow, 10am.

And there was another address.

"Sebastian?"

"Hmm?" I quickly folded the note and stuffed it into

my pocket before turning.

Neil stood in the doorway.

I was taken aback by his presence. "Second time in two days?"

"Guess so." Neil bent to set his forensic kit down.

I looked over his shoulder, but everyone in the shop was too far away to make out. Neil was staring at me when I turned my attention to him again. "Hi."

"Hey."

"I'm not sure what you're expecting to fingerprint for. My landlord already admitted to sneaking in, and he put this lovely specimen in my office—"

"So you're dating Winter."

"Uh, yes, it would appear that way."

"Why?"

"I like him," I awkwardly replied.

"You said when we broke up that you weren't going after him."

Was Neil… *jealous*?

Calvin really had been serious about Neil not being over me. Not that I had believed his whole alpha attitude of "I'm fucking you, you belong to me" had been unprovoked, but still. This didn't strike me as a behavior Neil would ever exhibit, but maybe in all the years we'd been dating, he'd hid a lot more of himself in the closet than just his sexuality.

Perhaps I had never really known him as intimately as I believed.

"I wasn't, but shit happened," I answered.

Like gunfights in the streets, as if New York City were the Wild West.

"And now you are," he finished.

"Now I am, yeah."

"Do you love him?"

"Neil, what the—"

"*Do you?*"

"I'm not talking to you about my relationship with Calvin," I said, holding up a hand.

"You cheated on me, Seb."

"You. Walked. Out. It was over."

"Over because I told you to watch your ass and you didn't."

"Oh, fuck you, Neil."

"But I see your new boyfriend lets you play detective with him," Neil continued. "I hope you're enjoying yourself. Do you get a good pounding every time you find a clue?" he asked, pointing at the mermaid on my desk.

"Stop it!"

This wasn't the same man I used to be in a relationship with. This man was angry and bitter and—

"I know you, Sebastian," Neil said quietly. "I know you're curious to a fault. You're willing to risk life and limb to fit together *puzzle pieces*."

"I do not."

"You're doing it now. How many more times do you have to be fed nonsensical bullshit before you admit how obsessed you are?"

"Is there a problem here, Detective Millett?" Calvin asked, standing behind us both just outside my office door.

Neil turned around. "No."

Calvin slowly took his eyes off Neil and directed his gaze at me. "Come on."

"The mermaid is here," I pointed out.

Calvin didn't say anything, but he didn't have to. What I saw worried me.

The stress was back.

He'd been really wound up since Ricky's. Okay, granted, I'm sure having to shoot a guy because your dumbass boyfriend was in danger probably didn't sit well, but he was usually so sure of everything when he was at work. Work-mode meant Calvin was untouchable.

Except recently, I had reason to believe that was not the case. That his armor had finally become too heavy and he couldn't breathe. God… how much worse had I made it? How could I have been so fucking stupid to not see that Calvin was finally losing his battle?

The look on his face… no one would know, but it was that same desperate and lost expression he got after coming down from a panic episode. That look of hopelessness Calvin always had about him as he recalled the faces of lives lost, of deaths he considered his fault.

"Never mind," I said, brushing by Neil. "We'll go. I'm not going to fight."

Calvin swallowed painfully and nodded.

I shot a look over my shoulder at Neil as I left. The look of contempt on his face made my stomach roll.

CHAPTER TEN

Pop and I ate Indian takeout for dinner.

He didn't know what he wanted to cook, and I was lying facedown on the couch, being a completely useless shit.

"So what's up?" Pop asked as we sat at the table, finishing our food.

"The ceiling, the sky, the clouds…."

"And what else?"

I frowned and stopped pushing the last of my rice around. "Can I put on music? I've got a hankering for some Ella." I stood before Pop answered and went to the record player that was part of his entertainment system. I turned it on before plucking one of the Ella Fitzgerald records from my dad's collection.

"Sebastian?" He turned in his chair.

I glanced at Pop before putting the record on, gently setting the needle down, and then letting Ella's perfect voice fill the room. I picked up the record sleeve and stared at her face. I never did have that rhythm she said I needed to give everything to.

"Kiddo," Pop prodded again.

"Calvin's not doing so well," I answered, and as I said that, I felt like I was betraying him.

Pop set his napkin down and got to his feet. He walked across the room, took the record sleeve and set it aside, before guiding me over to the couch. He sighed as he sat down beside me, knees cracking. "Did something happen?"

I guess I couldn't exactly tell him the shit that I did without Pop wanting to ground me from leaving the house like I were fourteen again.

I shrugged. "It's just… I think his partner is worried about him. He's been working hard lately, and I assumed it was some big cases, but she said they've been working on cold cases."

"Those are still important, though, aren't they?"

"Sure, but—" I looked down at my hands. I was gripping them hard without noticing. "He had one of his episodes at a diner, a few days ago. And I had to sit in the bathroom with him while he cried." I felt my own eyes begin to tear up. "Dad," I whispered, and it was hard to talk. "I'm more worried about him than anything. He's so stressed out from work, and I don't know why he's killing himself over it."

"You have to talk to him, Sebastian," Pop said, taking one of my hands and giving it a comforting squeeze.

I shook my head. "We can't. Every time I try—every fucking time—he gets so defensive."

"He's likely seen a lot of atrocities," Pop murmured. "Those didn't stay behind after he came home from the war. And he sees awful things like it right here in New York. I can understand the desire to bury it, to just shut it out, but the two of you won't make it if you can't find some way to talk."

"We have to make it," I said quickly, looking at him. "Dad. Calvin, he's… there's never been anyone like him. He gets my frustrating humor. He thinks I'm sexy, and how many goddamn times have you heard someone say *that* about me?"

"Sebastian."

"He likes to spoil me for no reason. Last week he came by the Emporium with my favorite coffee and cookies on his lunch break. I asked him what the occasion was, and he said, 'It's Tuesday.' Who does that? He likes watching silent films, and he lets me talk his ear off about stupid antique shit I know he doesn't find as interesting as I do.

"I need to return the affection. I mean—I *do*. Every chance I get. But I want to help him. I want to help him sleep through the night without dreaming about the dead children in Afghanistan he's convinced died because he wasn't a good enough soldier. I want him to stop crying, to stop being afraid. He's the bravest and strongest man I know, and he thinks the exact opposite of himself."

Everything poured out of me so fast, I had to come back up to breathe.

Pop let go of my hand, nodding. "And he won't go to a therapist?"

"No. And Quinn knows. Enough at least to be aware that there's reason for concern now." I took my glasses off and dabbed the corners of my eyes. "I don't want him to lose his job. He loves being a detective. It's what he's made for. But this can't keep going."

"What I said about him getting a dog…," my dad said after a pause. "I was serious."

"I know. I sort of suggested it too. But wouldn't he

have to go to a doctor first? I know he *needs* a doctor, but if it's official… his career…."

"I have a friend," Pop said. "She runs a nonprofit that trains rescue dogs to service vets. They're even taught how to wake owners from nightmares. They're not affiliated with the government or the VA—they help a lot of folks through donation alone."

"Really? They're in New York?"

"They have a small office here, yes. I can give her a call. Maybe you'd like to meet her before going to Calvin with the information?"

I did, actually. It sounded promising. Calvin was so opposed to visiting a VA hospital, but maybe I had to come at this nightmare from a different angle. How he'd have the time to care for a dog, I didn't know, but I was honest when I said I'd help. And if he benefited from this pup, maybe it would lower his stress and anxiety to a point that he'd not be opposed to at least talking now and then with a therapist.

I took a deep breath and nodded, feeling like a weight had been lifted from my chest. "Yeah, let's do that. Thanks, Pop."

"Sure thing, kiddo. You know I really like Calvin. And I love seeing how happy he makes you. We'll figure this out."

"I'm nominating you for Dad of the Year."

"Oh please," he said, standing. "I've got so many awards, they cut me off."

I laughed and nodded. "True. You are a pretty cool dad."

"Very hip," he confirmed, dating himself by word usage alone. "I need to take Maggie on a walk. Want to come along?"

"Sure, I—"

The building's front door buzzer went off.

"Was Calvin coming back here after work?" Pop asked as he went and hit the door-lock button.

I turned from my seat on the couch as he unlocked the apartment door. "I wasn't under the impression he was."

Pop opened it when there was a gentle knock. "Hello there, Calvin. We were just talking about you."

"Good evening, William," Calvin said quietly. He stepped inside when my dad ushered him in. Calvin turned and looked at me. "Hey."

"Hey back."

Calvin stuffed his hands in his coat pockets. "Can we talk?"

This was… not a good sign. Nothing good ever comes when the person you're dating says you've got to *talk*.

My heart started pounding harder as I stood. "Yeah. Of course."

My dad immediately grabbed his coat. "I'll leave you boys to it. Come on, Maggie," he called, and dad's princess ran to the door. "I'll be back in, oh… twenty minutes or so," he said, giving me a knowing nod before him and Maggie left.

Calvin didn't move.

Something was very wrong.

I walked slowly around the couch, standing just far enough away that it felt strange. "Cal? Look, before you say anything, let me apologize. I was stupid. *I know*. But I didn't… realize what I must have put you through today."

"You mean the part where you nearly had your skull smashed in?"

I nodded. "That would be the part," I whispered.

He looked away, staring at the entertainment system.

When had Ella stopped singing? I hadn't noticed.

"Baby…," he said quietly, sort of trailing off.

"I want you to stop working so much," I blurted out. Calvin looked back at me.

I nodded furiously and balled my hands into fists. "As soon as we started dating, you went into work overdrive. I thought you had big cases and bosses breathing down your neck, but after Quinn told me differently? She's worried about you too, Calvin. You're working yourself to death, and I don't… want to lose you. Not for a long goddamn time, do you hear me? I'm talking canes and liver spots and pants hiked up to our chests."

Calvin didn't speak. He shifted his weight slightly from one foot to the other, but otherwise, not a response.

"I want to spend time with you," I continued. "And I get that you have a demanding job, and that you love what you do. But to find out that you stay late, don't sleep or eat, when you have the opportunity to come home? We don't have to do *anything*. You want to de-stress by eating takeout and watching hockey and nothing more—I'm down. Let's do it. I'm not a needy guy. My only request is that you don't kill yourself."

"The same could be said about you, Sebastian," Calvin said suddenly.

"What?"

"Any regular person, after nearly getting blown up, would let the police do their fucking job," he snapped. "But not you. You've got to be Sherlock."

"This isn't about my dumb choices, Calvin. I'm being serious!"

"So am I." Calvin moved forward, and as he got close and I could make out his features better, I realized how pissed he was. "I had to shoot a man today because of you."

"He's fine. And not a good guy, anyway. He tried to kill that poor girl."

Calvin jabbed his finger against my chest. "I shot him because of *you*. When I ran into that club, I didn't know if you were dead or alive. I couldn't fucking *breathe*, Sebastian. It was like every fear I had was coming true. I told you how scared I was. Of us—of something happening to you because of *us*."

"Ricky didn't stop to ask if I enjoyed cock."

"No, but Luther North had some fucking opinions. This man has threatened you and is still suspect numero uno in the murder of Meredith Brown," Calvin said forcefully.

"This isn't about either of us being gay, Calvin. *It's not*. It's not about holding hands in public. Jesus Christ. I could blow you in public and no one would even consider trying to piss you off. This is about you and your mental health. Construe it how you want, but your PTSD is fucking destroying you and it's breaking my heart!"

Calvin's expression dropped, the crease in his brow softening. His jaw muscles were tense. "Didn't I say it was inevitable?" he asked, all at once very tired-sounding.

I shook my head in confusion before I understood what he meant.

Calvin's reluctance toward dating to begin with was because of his PTSD. He was convinced he'd *break my heart*.

"No," I said firmly. I grabbed the front of his jacket and pulled him closer. "It's not the same thing, and you damn well know it. It hurts me because I—Calvin. I love you so much, it's like I've outdone the Grinch. My heart has grown a hundred sizes, and it's still not big enough to hold my love for you. That shit is fucking pouring out all over the place, and it's sappy and stupid and people are probably sick to death of hearing me talk about you."

Calvin's eyes were shiny, and he took a strangled breath. "First time you've said it."

"Is it? I've sure as hell thought it."

He snorted and laughed. "Yeah, honey. First time."

"My apology."

"Apology accepted."

"Can we kiss and make up?"

He nodded.

"And talk about you."

"I don't want to talk about—"

"Then no kissing and no making up."

"God…. Sebastian."

"I'm serious. I'm not backing down this time. Fight me all you want, but I can't watch you lose this battle alone. I know that I won't ever really understand what you've experienced and what you've seen, and if you can't talk to me about those memories, that's okay. But I'm in this for the long haul, and if you're afraid to seek help alone, we'll do it together."

Calvin was frowning, but he took my face into his hands and stroked my cheek with his thumb. "You are such a pain in my ass," he muttered.

"No, I'd make it feel good."

Calvin laughed again.

"This is why people try to kill me," I pointed out.

"Don't joke."

"Too soon?"

"Yes."

I stood up on my toes, closed the distance between us, and kissed Calvin, sweet and innocent, just a little peck on his lips. "I'll stop being a detective."

"Why do I not believe you?" he murmured against my mouth, kissing me again.

"You're a realist."

"Are your fingers crossed?"

"Umm-hmm…."

Calvin held me firmer, kissing me longer. "You frustrate the hell out of me, sweetie."

"Good." I stepped back and took Calvin's big hands into mine. "Let's talk about dogs."

"What? Again?"

"Again."

Calvin didn't speak.

I let go, tugged his jacket off, and tossed it onto a chair. "Stay awhile."

"I have to go back soon."

"Were you here for this fight we just had?" I asked.

"I don't have cold cases now."

"Fine. But come sit first." I pulled him around the side of the couch. "Don't get angry, but—I told Pop."

"About what?" Calvin asked hesitantly.

"About you. And this," I said, waving a hand absently.

"Sebastian, are you serious?"

"Just listen," I said, holding on to his shoulders and staring at him. Calvin was not happy. "He knows a woman who runs a group. They supply trained dogs to people with PTSD, anxiety, all that sort of stuff, and he said they help a lot of vets. *And*—" I continued when he opened his mouth to speak. "They're not part of any government organization. We don't have to go to a VA hospital or anything like that."

"Why do you want me to have a dog?" Calvin looked frustrated, but managing to even ask one question that kept the conversation going was a plus.

"Pop says that dogs are good for people who need a

little help. Look at it this way… a dog isn't going to judge you. And you can talk to them."

"Talk to a dog," he stated, not amused.

"Yeah. If you wanted to get something off your chest but you couldn't say it to me, a dog will listen and not say anything that you don't want to hear."

"Talking to a dog isn't going to make me feel better."

"How do you know?"

Calvin shook his head and let out a heavy sigh.

I took his hands into mine and squeezed them. "Pop said these dogs are even trained to wake people from bad dreams, Calvin. That would help you. If they could stop the dream before it becomes too much and interrupts what little sleep you get…."

Calvin rubbed my knuckles with his thumb while staring at the floor. "When I work," he whispered, "there isn't time for anything else."

"I know."

"But since I met you, Seb…. All I think about is you. And it's like you're not a safe topic for my brain. I focus on you more and more, and it just brings everything to the surface. I don't know why," Calvin said with a shaky breath. He let go and put a hand over his mouth.

I knew why.

Because he was finally happy. Calvin was terrified of losing that.

And loss was what haunted him, even before me.

"I need to keep working," he said after clearing his throat and taking the reins of his emotions under control again.

I shook my head. "We have to find a healthy medium. And we will, I swear." I reached out and turned his face to me. "Would you mind if I at least met this woman tomorrow?"

Calvin hesitated but eventually shook his head. "I don't mind," he finally answered.

"Good God, look at the progress we're making."

Calvin smiled.

"I love your smile. It brightens your whole face up."

"Does it? I feel like I've been run over by a semi."

I kissed Calvin again.

This was a turning point for us.

He ran his fingers through my hair, gripping a handful as he deepened the kiss. Calvin's tongue touched mine and sent waves of pleasure down my spine. Our rough jaws scraped, and the added texture had chills of excitement going straight to my cock.

I heard an embarrassing moan escape my throat.

"You okay?" Calvin whispered.

"Fine. Apparently just in dire need."

"Your father is coming back soon."

"Don't care." I sat up, kissing Calvin again as I moved to sit on his lap, a knee on either side of his hips.

Calvin groaned against my mouth, his hands running down my back. They stopped at my jeans, and he slipped his fingers in, groping what he could reach.

"Cal," I said, nipping his lip and moving to kiss along his jaw and down his neck.

"Yeah, baby?"

"I want it the other way."

He growled playfully and brought his hands around to knead me through the denim. "You want *what* the other way?"

"Don't tease."

"You like being teased."

I leaned over to kiss him hard. "I want to fuck you."

"Yeah," he whispered, nodding. "I want that. I've been waiting for you to bury your cock in me."

It wasn't something I did very much of—and with Neil, all of one time—but every once in a while, I was feeling extra frisky. Calvin had such a perfect ass too. Freckled and muscular and begging to be fucked.

"You should have asked," I said, pressing my forehead to his.

Calvin reached under my shirt and trailed his blunt fingertips along my heated skin. "I like it when you're confident in what you want. It's a turn-on."

"Everything about you turns me on," I countered.

Maggie barked from outside the apartment door.

Calvin turned his head and took his hands off me. "Rain check."

"Christ, I need my own place again." I rolled off his lap and sprawled out across the couch. I glanced down, my hard-on not getting the message that playtime was over, and I hastily tugged a nearby blanket from the other night over me.

"Now it's more obvious," Calvin pointed out.

"Shh...."

The front door opened, and Maggie and Pop came back inside. Pop took the leash off Maggie. "How's everything?"

"Good." I tilted my head back to see him staring curiously while removing his coat. "What?"

"Why do you have the blanket over your lap? *Oh*."

"Oh my God," I groaned.

"Not on my couch," Pop said sternly.

"We didn't do anything on the couch, Dad."

"Only because I came back. If I find any stains—"

"Dad," I whined.

Calvin smiled as he stood, adjusted his tie and suit coat, and then tapped my foot. "I have to go."

"Already?"

He nodded.

I sighed and pushed the blanket off before standing. "Coming back?"

"I'll probably go to my place."

"Probably?"

"I *will* go to my place," Calvin confirmed. "I'll sleep."

"All right." I wrapped my arms around his neck and hugged Calvin tight. "Be safe."

He murmured in agreement, petting the back of my head before kissing my forehead. "I'll call you tomorrow. Nothing stupid, got it?"

"Have you met me?"

Calvin grunted. "I should know better." He let go of me and grabbed his coat as he walked to the door. "William," he said, pausing to shake my dad's hand, because Calvin was always a gentleman. "Have a good night."

"You too, Calvin."

Calvin patted Maggie's head before walking out the door.

Pop turned to me. "So?"

"Let's go meet some dogs tomorrow."

The dogs were a bust.

K4V—K9s for Vets—may not have been affiliated with the VA or received funding from the government, but part of the application process still required veterans to have their PTSD diagnosed and verified by a doctor.

Which Calvin hadn't and wouldn't do.

Gwen Sutton, the owner of the organization, did let me meet the dogs at least. I think she felt bad for me.

"Hey," I said when Calvin answered his phone. "I just wanted to let you know that I met the person who runs the K9s for Vets program."

"How'd it go?" he asked, sounding quiet and wary.

"She's nice. The dogs were all cool. She started the organization because her brother came back from Afghanistan with PTSD. Her name's Gwen. She really wants to meet you."

"Why's that?"

"I guess you and her brother were deployed at the same time. Maybe you knew him."

"There were a lot of soldiers in Afghanistan."

I shrugged to myself. I was standing outside of a little restaurant a few blocks from the K4V office. Pop was waiting inside. "Anyway. I think you'd enjoy checking the place out. The application process is pretty straightforward. It's basically like adopting a normal dog. With just… one extra thing."

"What *thing*?" Calvin echoed.

I steeled myself. "Vets have to have a note from their doctors."

He didn't answer.

"Yeah," I said to his silence. "I figured. But I thought you should know."

"Now I know," he concluded.

Calvin 1, Sebastian 0.

Back to the beginning.

"Anyway. I won't keep you."

"Bye, sweetie."

"Bye." I pulled the phone away and sighed.

The call ended and the time flashed on the screen: 9:30 a.m. Did I have somewhere to be besides breakfast with Pop?

I frowned and tugged the restaurant door open. I walked down the aisles of little tables before sitting across from Pop.

He set his glass of juice down and gave me the Dad-Look. "No?"

I shook my head. "No," I echoed. "I've barely managed to convince Cal to start talking to *me* about everything. He's not ready for a therapist, which means he's left undiagnosed and untreated. Which means no dog from Gwen," I concluded. I flipped the menu pages maybe a bit harder than necessary.

"He's scared, Sebastian. Be patient."

"I know, I know," I said while looking back up at Pop. "I'm just worried."

He nodded and pulled his cell out. Pop held it far away and tilted his chin up, reading like he needed to wear bifocals. He started typing.

"Want to borrow my glasses?" I teased.

"Ha, ha. I can see just fine, mister."

"Okay, but just so you know, this one is sugar and this is salt," I said while reaching over to hold up the shakers from the tabletop.

Pop paused whatever he was doing to give me the hairy eyeball. "Thin ice, kiddo."

I grinned widely. "You love me."

"Uh-huh." He finished typing and set the phone aside.

"What's up?"

"Oh, nothing. Asking Jeanie at Puppy Pals for a favor." One of the many shelters my dad volunteered at.

I was about to ask what sort of favor this mysterious Jeanie was doing for my father, when I suddenly remembered where I had to be. "Fuck!" I reached into my pockets quickly, fishing out the congratulatory note from yesterday.

Visitors needed a guide to Thebes. Tomorrow, 10am.

After the heart-to-heart with Calvin yesterday, I had all but forgotten the second address.

"What's wrong?" Pop asked.

"No, it's fine," I said while quickly standing. "I just remembered I have somewhere to be."

"Where? You didn't order any food yet," Pop replied.

"It's fine. I'll grab something in a bit." I moved around the table to lean down and give him a hug. "I'll see you soon. Love you!" I called while moving away.

"Bye, kiddo."

I all but ran out the door and hailed the nearest taxi.

Off to the Met.

CHAPTER ELEVEN

Another museum.

I don't know why this psycho was ruining locations that I deeply adored, but I was not happy about the prospect of finding another body in an exhibit. And this clue was pretty obvious.

Come on—*Thebes*?

The Met's Egyptian exhibits.

Now the real question was, where would I find the grisly evidence I had been readying myself for the entire taxi ride there? The Egyptian wing of the Metropolitan Museum of Art was enormous. I'd spent entire days in the past never migrating to the other half of the museum, simply because there was so much to see and read about in the Egyptian section.

It was Saturday morning, and despite the doors just opening, the museum was already proving it would be a busy day. At least it would be bustling with tourists and not kids on school field trips. Trying to navigate around a group of thirty twelve-year-olds who had no desire to be there and had never been told to be quiet in a museum was one of my short fuses.

I bought my ticket and pushed by some of the other people entering the Egyptian wing, ignoring their protests. Sorry, people, amateur sleuth on a case. I didn't have time to be courteous.

The first exhibit in Gallery 100 was the Mastaba Tomb of Perneb. Small and cramped, sure, but you could actually get inside the building so someone could have shoved a body in there.

Nothing on the left—shit—nothing in the right corner either. I hurried back out and turned to stare up at the structure. To the right was the start of ancient Egypt; to the left was the history of the kingdom once the Romans came. I shut my eyes and thought about both halls and what sort of areas could conceal a body.

And not an ancient one wrapped in bandages.

I decided to start at the beginning and ran to the right hall. A security guard called me sir and ordered that I walk.

I played with fire by walking briskly.

It was hard not to stop and examine the artifacts, statues, and structures as I made my way down the twisting galleries, but I had to find this clue before the museum filled up with people and an unfortunate out-of-towner found a dead guy before I did.

I pulled out my phone as I made my way past displays of jewelry and textiles. "Calvin," I said when he picked up. "I'm making a preemptive call."

"What did you do?"

"Nothing yet. Do you always think I'm up to something?"

"I'd say no if I didn't know better."

"I feel no love."

"Seb."

"I'm at the Met."

He cursed under his breath.

"Look, I didn't even remember until this morning. Last night threw me for a spin, you know? But the mermaid—there was another note. It had this address and mentioned some garbage about Thebes, so I'm making my way through the Egyptian wing."

"Sebastian, stop right now and turn back. It's too—"

"Dangerous?" I supplied before he could. "There's a security guard in every room. I haven't found anything yet, but I think you should come now. If this is anything like the other day, give me ten more minutes and I'll trip over a corpse."

"I should have arrested you back in December when I had the chance."

"I love you too."

"I'll be there soon."

I hung up and stuffed my cell back into my pocket, stopping in a side room full of coffins and more linens. My knowledge of ancient Egypt was limited at best, but Thebes was where the Valley of the Kings was—the final resting ground for nobles and pharaohs. So maybe the clue was kind of like the whale, and I should be looking more at death artifacts?

But a tour through this room, checking inside the empty coffins on display, proved futile. At least with the natural history museum, the body had been tucked into the one area not carefully concealed to keep the public out. A body inside a coffin or sarcophagus would make sense, but there was no way to get around the glass walls protecting them.

It was practically empty this deep into the exhibit.

People meandered through the dozens of rooms with no reason to rush. I stepped into the next room—the Sackler Wing. The north wall was glass, the morning light shining through. The ceiling soared overhead, and in the middle on display was the Temple of Dendur, surrounded by a reflection pool. The room was actually quite lovely, the water meant to reflect the Nile River and the sloping wall an interpretation of the cliffs of the original location in Egypt.

One security guard was walking lazily down the hall ahead of me, and one visitor was studying some statues on my immediate right. I had gone through the entire Egyptian exhibit—albeit in a rush—but not found any reasonable location for hiding a body. Except… what about the temple? It was certainly big enough….

I walked along the side of the reflection pool toward the steps that led up to the structure. Even though it wasn't a particularly sunny day, the glare on the surface of the water was already making my eyes hurt. I had to look away and study the far wall ahead, so I nearly walked right by the body floating in the water.

Nearly.

I jumped backward in fright, even though I had been fully prepared to come upon a dead person. I stared at it from several feet away. It just floated lazily on its stomach, facedown in the still water. I know the museum just opened, but had no one seriously noticed this yet? I mean, it was *right there*. In the open. I figured I'd at least find the poor bastard crammed into some nook.

I took a few steps forward.

Most likely a man, with short, dark hair and a cheap, dark-colored suit. Something was stuck to his back, and when I got closer and leaned over the water, it appeared to be a scrap of paper inside a plastic sleeve.

Fuck. Just like the mermaid advertisement at the

other museum.

I reached out, shaking hand peeling the clue off the dead man's back. "Stop right there!"

I startled and stumbled a few steps back, dropping the plastic sleeve. I let out a breath as several uniformed officers were heading my way. "You guys scared the piss out of me."

"Sir, I'm going to have to ask you to move back and put your hands on the wall," one officer said, hand resting on his weapon.

"Whoa, whoa, wait. Where's Detective Winter? I called him."

"Sir, against the wall right now," the officer said again.

I took a few steps back as instructed but didn't turn in surrender. "I didn't kill that guy," I protested, pointing at the floater. "I literally just found him."

Another officer was approaching me. His face looked like he'd gotten into plenty of scraps in his lifetime and he knew how to play dirty if it came to that. He ordered me to put my hands up in a deep, booming voice.

The first policeman pulled his pistol.

I put my goddamn hands up. "This is a mistake," I said as brute number two began to frisk me for weapons. He pulled my cell from my pocket, my magnifying glass, and the note about Thebes. "There. See? Not even a toothpick."

"Stand down, officers," ordered a third voice.

I turned in the direction I had come from, Calvin and Quinn slowly coming into focus. I waved awkwardly. "Hi."

"Mr. Snow is not a suspect," Calvin said firmly. "Hand over his possessions."

I took my things back from Broken Nose. "So," I

said, nodding my head at the body. "Found it."

"This is becoming absurd," Calvin said under his breath.

"How long is this going to keep up?" Quinn asked, crossing her arms.

I shrugged. "For as long as this killer has P.T. Barnum artifacts to dish out as grand prizes?" I gave Calvin yesterday's message. "I'm sorry I came here in a rush without talking to you first, but the note said 10:00 a.m. I thought if I waited, other patrons would stumble upon—er—him first."

Calvin took a breath. "So. If this is anything like the other day, the identity of this man may lead to him being a cold case suspect."

"Wanted for murder," I added.

"That Sebastian has to solve," Quinn concluded.

Calvin swore, shaking his head. "Sebastian is not solving *anything*. This has to stop."

"Cal—"

"No," he said over me. "You receive a threat, find a murdered person, solve it, only to be handed another threat. The cycle has to stop here and now."

"Can I at least check the note?"

"What note?"

I pointed to the floor. "It was taped to his back."

"And you touched it," Calvin concluded.

I motioned with my hand. "Just a little."

He let out a deep breath and reached into his pocket to pull out a pen. Calvin walked to the soggy, plastic sleeve on the floor, and crouched down beside it.

I followed him and got down, holding out my magnifying glass. "I don't know how anyone read print so small back then," I stated, getting low to the floor.

"What is it?" Calvin reluctantly asked.

"I think it's a clipping from maybe a brochure?" I got onto my knees and leaned over the paper, since I knew Calvin would protest me touching it further. "A Mummy from Thebes," I read aloud. "Which now presents itself to the visitor."

"What's that mean?"

I shook my head. "I don't know. Some of it is hard to make out—oh wait. It's definitely P.T.-related. At the bottom of the paragraph, it thanks Mr. Barnum. Can you flip it over? Last time, there was a note on the back."

Calvin reached out with his pen and turned the sleeve over. "Solve the murder, win a book."

"Great," I grumbled. "The last book I was involved with was quite enough, thank you."

"What book would this be suggesting?"

I was thoughtful for a moment, considering the wording that described a mummy from Thebes and the small drawing that had appeared to be a bandaged body inside a coffin, although the quality wasn't great. "I think it might be *Barnum's American Museum illustrated*. It was a guidebook that patrons could purchase when they visited the museum."

"It is rare?"

"Most definitely. The Library of Congress lists a copy as part of their Rare Book and Special Collections Division, if I recall. Plus, it covers in detail a number of the items that perished in the fire. Some we may have otherwise never known about. Newspapers of the time reported the death of live animals and the loss of artifacts belonging to the Founding Fathers, but there was so much more. Taxidermy—which you'd be surprised what that's worth—Roman urns, Native American weapons, suits of armor—there's even some advertisements for local businesses at the beginning. I love old ads."

"You're a walking encyclopedia, Seb."

"It's my job."

"That it is," Calvin said dryly. "And yet here you are." He looked at me.

"Let me help," I said quietly. "Whoever is behind this, they're doing it to get my attention."

"If I had been thirty seconds later getting to Ricky's, you might not be here, baby."

I swallowed. "Yeah, but—look, even when I was keeping my nose to the ground, someone blew my apartment up. This isn't going to stop on its own, so let me do what I can."

Calvin let out a held breath, not breaking eye contact.

"Wouldn't you feel better knowing exactly what I was doing instead of me sneaking around?"

"Nice try."

"Come on."

"You're not a cop."

"No, but I am a busybody who gets lucky now and then."

Calvin rolled his eyes to the ceiling.

I stood, looking down at him. "Let me at least stay long enough to see who the victim is."

I had to admit, I was surprised when Calvin agreed to let me stay. The Sackler Wing was shut down and soon had a number of officers, a medical examiner, and—surprise, surprise—my ex-favorite CSU detective. Neil saw me, we made awkward eye contact, and then he set his kit down and busied himself rifling through the contents. I pushed away from the wall I was standing at and came up behind

Quinn and Calvin, who were watching as the body was being removed from the reflection pool and laid on the floor to be photographed.

"What do you think?" Quinn murmured.

"Didn't drown," Calvin replied as he stepped forward to speak with the examiner.

I moved to stand where he had been. "How do you know he didn't drown?" I asked Quinn.

"See how his head was turned to the side? Even in something this shallow, if the person dies in the water, the body tends to lay on its stomach, head and arms down. If they died on land and rigor begins to set in, you can see the unnatural position even after the body is removed from the water."

"I bet he was shot," I muttered. "Why he'd be tossed in the pool after, who knows."

"Maybe our suspect wanted to be sure you found him," Quinn replied. She looked away when a uniformed officer called her from the temple display.

"Quinn—"

"Hold that thought," she said before walking up the stairs and leaving me.

They'd probably found where the victim had been killed. If rigor had set in, there was likely at least *some* blood at the scene of the crime. What a bitch it would be to clean those ancient stones of some poor bastard's arterial spray.

I remained where I was, watching everyone around me go about their job in a sort of detached, professional manner. Calvin always said motive wasn't what was most important. It was his job to gather the facts and make an arrest based on what was available to him. I tended to disagree. This wasn't a crime of passion or opportunity. This was methodical, planned, and staged. There was reason behind these deaths, even if it were ghastly and made no sense to someone of a sane mind. I firmly believed that if we didn't at least try to understand the motive the killer found to be a rational reason to off people, we were only looking at half of the picture.

And yet, even as I racked my brain, I couldn't understand what anyone would gain from this. The antiques involved were bizarre, yes, but they definitely had monetary value. And yet, the suspect was giving them to me as a job well done for solving a cold case. So they weren't looking for cash, and they weren't even trying to keep the items for themselves.

What remained? What was constant?

Me. I was always in the thick of it.

And why? Because I wanted to be here. I wanted to be smart and clever and piece together real-life puzzles. I just *couldn't* walk away from something only partially solved.

Of course, our mystery killer knew this about me. Everything was so carefully organized and addressed to me. Perhaps I was a scapegoat? What if sooner or later I was going to find myself in a situation where I had to kill or be killed—what if I were playing right into what somebody wanted from the start?

I am not a smart man….

I swallowed hard and tried to calm the nervous flipping that my gut was beginning to do.

Okay, so whether or not that was the motive or reason or plan behind all this, it still didn't confirm who was behind it.

Someone who knew me.

Someone who clearly didn't like me.

Luther North was still Grade-A prime suspect to me. The shithead had keys to my shop, had already admitted to breaking in to plant the mermaid—who's to say he hadn't planted the bricks? He knew where I lived too. And he definitely wasn't a BFF. At most he tolerated me. He had to. I was under lease and followed the rules. He may not have liked me, but trying to kick me out of the shop because he thought gay guys were icky was grounds for a lawsuit, and Luther wasn't *that* stupid. He could have made up that shit about the cop that threatens via text.

Neil shoved me on his way by just then, looking over his shoulder while hiking up the stairs to the temple.

And then there was that guy. Not that I suspected Neil of killing people. Because I had *not* dated a psychopath for four years.

He was just pissed.

Instead of getting away from me after a bad breakup, he had not only Calvin—but me as well—shoved in his face. I could see why anyone would be upset from that.

Except....

The completely insane, illogical, I-must-be-drunk-or-something part of my mind said: it's possible.

It wasn't.

No. It absolutely *was not* possible.

But the facts were still the same as they were in December. Neil knew where I lived. He knew where I worked, how to get around the cameras—and as a forensic detective, he for sure must have known a way to bypass security systems. And even more than Luther, Neil knew *me*. He knew my habits and tendencies.

If I were playing into the killer's hands and getting myself involved in something I didn't quite understand yet, they knew the way to keep me active in the game. They knew to keep me curious—just like P.T. Barnum had done with his crowds of museum patrons.

Neil knows I'm a curious shit.

What if Luther wasn't making up that crap about a cop threatening him?

I mean…. Neil was a cop.

I shook my head and balled my hands into fists to hold them against my temple. I wasn't being smart about this. I was taking the evidence and suspects I had and forcing them to fit.

Right?

Because this was nuts.

Neil wasn't handling a breakup well. That didn't mean he lost his fucking mind and turned into a murderer.

"Hey."

I looked up so fast, I nearly got whiplash. Calvin was staring at me, those pretty and intense gray eyes burning a hole right through me. "What?" I asked, trying to sound casual.

"Something wrong?"

I swallowed and looked over Calvin's shoulder, watching Neil go into the temple. "No. I don't think so."

He turned briefly in the direction I was looking before meeting my gaze again.

Was Calvin having the same thoughts I was?

"Come here," he said with a nod of his head toward the pool.

I followed close behind him, resisting the desire to grab his hand and let his strength ground me. I took a deep breath and peered at the waterlogged body before us. "So he was killed in the temple?"

Calvin looked at me curiously.

"Well, Neil wouldn't be collecting evidence in the temple otherwise."

Calvin didn't have a response.

I looked back down at the dead guy. His face and

hands were kind of bloated. He'd probably been dead since at least yesterday for rigor to set in, but also enough time in the water for his skin to be reacting like that. I didn't want to say he was familiar—because in life he'd have certainly been less gross-looking—but the nagging feeling that I had met him before persisted.

"Sebastian?" Calvin asked quietly.

I looked up briefly. "I think I might know him. I mean, not *know*, but met him once before…. He tried to sell me shit once upon a time."

The medical examiner pulled out a soggy wallet from the back pocket of the man's pants and offered it to Calvin.

Calvin quickly put on some gloves, accepted it, and briefly searched the contents. "Richard Newell, Brooklyn."

"Got a museum ID here, Detective," the examiner said as he pulled a badge free and held it up.

Richard Newell of Brooklyn, working security for the Met.

"Son of a bitch," Calvin said quietly to himself.

"Cold case?"

He nodded with a bit of reluctance. "Yes. One that has been unsolved since before I joined homicide. The detective on the case had tunnel vision."

"What do you mean?"

"He was so sure of his person of interest that he didn't seem to even consider other evidence." Calvin motioned to Richard. "Four years ago a man working in acquisitions here at the museum was found dead in Central Park. It was gruesome. Personal. The detective on the case uncovered that he had been stealing artifacts from the museum, and it was suspected that he had been working with another staff member."

"Richard?" I concluded.

"That's what I think. From what I've uncovered, the victim—Earl Franklin—put in a good word to get Richard the job. Richard had a juvenile record for theft."

"You don't think he changed his ways?"

"No. Not really. Something about the case always sat wrong with me," Calvin murmured.

"Who did the other detective suspect?"

"Earl's boss. Apparently they had had an on-and-off relationship that on its last off didn't end so well. The boss was found innocent by the courts, though."

I looked down at the late Richard. "So you think Richard and Earl were stealing together, maybe someone got greedy, and the end result was Earl's untimely demise?"

"That's about the long and short of it."

"And if this is like the other day, then our resident psycho killed Richard because he was guilty of murder and now wants me to prove it. Prove that he killed Earl, maybe."

Calvin shook his head. "This'll be a fucking trip to explain to my sergeant."

I stared at Richard again. "Were any of the stolen artifacts found?"

"A few that I know of. The FBI got involved at that point. Art Crime Team," Calvin clarified.

I perked up. "Do you think you could find out where they were recovered from? Or at least what the items were?" When Calvin stared at me expectantly, I said, "I have an idea. It might not lead to anything, but if you could let me know…."

"Sebastian."

"The antique community is small, just like any other specific interest. We talk to each other, so bad deals, theft, or forgery all come up. If memory serves me right, Richard here couldn't provide paperwork for the items he wanted to sell. Someone else must know about him."

CHAPTER TWELVE

Max almost knocked me over when he ran from the front door of the Emporium and crashed into me. He practically squeezed the life out of me with a hug. "Seb!"

"M-Max! God—can't breathe."

"How are you? *Are you okay*?" He pulled back and put his hands on my shoulders.

"I think you broke a rib."

"I'm so happy to be at work again."

"It's only because Calvin doesn't trust me alone."

Said redhead frowned and crossed his arms over his chest.

Max dropped his hands. "Are you still being a sleuth?"

"Yes, he is," Calvin supplied before I could speak.

"With police permission," I added.

Max made a face. "I'm not following."

"I'm making a few calls, with Calvin's approval."

"But he's not allowed to leave and sneak around," Calvin said.

"It's like house arrest without the fancy ankle jewelry," I finished.

"Very funny," Calvin muttered.

"So I have to babysit Seb?" Max asked Calvin. "You know, if he tells me to do something, I technically have to listen. He signs my paychecks."

"Don't worry about that," Calvin answered.

I pulled my phone out and checked the time. It was already after noon when Calvin finished at the Met and drove us over to the Emporium. "I should call Aubrey. I might be able to catch him on his lunch break."

"All right," Calvin answered. "But I'm serious. Tell me what you find out and stay here with Max."

"When do I get to go home?"

"I'll have someone pick you up. It's not safe to be alone right now. Understand?"

"Copy, Major."

Calvin pinched the bridge of his nose briefly. "I'm leaving." He leaned down and kissed me.

"Bye."

"Bye, sweetheart."

Max held his hand up and gave Calvin a high-five as he walked by and let himself out the front door. "So," he began. "We're calling Aubrey?"

"That's right." I walked up the steps to the register and went into my tiny office. I sat at the computer, powered it on, and then switched on the low-intensity lamp.

Max dragged a stool from the counter into the room and sat beside me. "So what's Aubs know that you don't?"

"Plenty," I said, signing into my account. I sniffed the air. "What's that smell?"

"Oh, life was getting a bit too normal, so I bought some pig guts and stuffed them under the floor," Max said with a shrug.

"You *what*?" I shouted.

He started laughing. "Chill, boss. I think that's my fish sandwich in the fridge from last Sunday."

"Gross. Toss that out before we leave tonight."

I signed on to Skype, leaned close to read the contacts list on the screen, and then called one. The program rang a few times, and Max made stupid faces at the webcam. "Stop," I grumbled.

"Sourpuss."

"Am not."

"Are too."

The ringing stopped and the receiver's webcam turned on to show the image of a hand adjusting the camera. Then Aubrey Grant sat back and smiled at the screen.

Aubrey is not the sort of guy one assumes to be remotely involved with the antiquing world. You come to expect older people or crotchety shits like myself. Aubrey looks like a kid, which made it all the more horrifying when I learned he was actually five years older than me. Dark eyes, dark eyebrows, but really light hair, which he explained was bleached white. He had a nose ring and those gauged ears too, which I didn't like but Max always complimented him on.

"Hey guys!" Aubrey said, waving at the screen. "Long time, no see."

"Seriously," Max answered. "When are you coming back to New York?"

"Maybe this summer for the antique fair at the Javits Center."

"Want to be my plus one?" Max asked, wiggling

his eyebrows.

Aubrey laughed. "I'll think about it."

"How's the island life?" I asked after shushing Max.

"Good. Hot as hell. I've got the AC running."

Aubrey lived in Key West and worked at one of the local historical homes. I'd always wanted to go down and visit the place, but outside of going on tours of old buildings, Key West didn't exactly appeal to me. I was definitely not a beach-goer, and just thinking about that much sun made my eyes ache.

"How's the urban jungle?" Aubrey asked in return.

"Rainy with a chance of murder."

Aubrey made a face and laughed awkwardly. "Come again?"

"Aubs," I said, unfolding a piece of paper from my pocket. Calvin had made a photocopy of Richard's driver's license and "accidentally" left it where I'd conveniently find it. "I know you've got some—er—history with the FBI guys who work in Art Crime...."

Aubrey pursed his lips together. "History with *a* guy. Don't make it sound like I fucked the entire lot of them."

"Right, sorry." I cleared my throat. "Does the name Richard Newell sound familiar?"

Aubrey's bitter expression slowly transitioned into one of thoughtfulness. "Hmm... should it?"

"I was hoping so. He might have been involved with a number of museum thefts. About four years ago. And possibly a murder."

"Jesus."

"My boyfriend says the FBI got involved."

"I knew this wasn't a house call when I saw your name."

"I don't mean to stir up unwanted memories, but

I was hoping you might know something. Calvin's a detective, but getting paperwork from the FBI is going to be a waiting game for him."

"Wait, who's Calvin?" Aubrey asked.

"Seb's new beau," Max provided.

"Stop it," I said.

"Congratulations."

"Thanks," I murmured. "About Richard?"

"Sebastian," Aubrey said with a sigh. "I wasn't even with my ex four years ago. And by the time I met Matt, he had transitioned to Organized Crime."

"Here, just look at a picture of the guy. I know I've met him in the past. And this is a small world—you could have met him too before you moved to America's retirement community."

"That's Fort Lauderdale."

"I thought that was spring break gone wild?"

Aubrey chuckled. "It's both."

"Florida is weird." I held up the photocopied picture to the webcam. "Can you see it?"

"I'll be damned."

"What?"

"I think I know the guy."

I lowered the picture so I could see Aubrey again. "Yeah?"

"He looks fatter—then again, show me one person with a flattering driver's license."

I turned the picture around to stare at it.

"I mean," Aubrey continued. "It's been a while, but when I used to work at the pawn shop in New York—that guy was on our wall."

"On your wall?" Max repeated in confusion.

Aubrey nodded. "Yeah. The 'don't serve these

assholes' wall. I can't entirely remember why, but he was probably trying to off something fake or of questionable origin." He tugged absently on one of his gauged ears. "He had the weirdest voice. Like he'd inhaled helium."

Max started laughing.

"Was he ever investigated by the FBI?"

"I don't know," Aubrey said. "How much do you think a government agent actually told me about his cases? Dating or not?"

"Maybe I've got a way of wooing information out of guys with badges," I replied.

"Seb harasses cops until they would rather divulge information than listen to one more minute of his pestering," Max said.

I was going to have to rethink this year's holiday bonus for Max. "Do you have any recollection as to what Richard may have been trying to sell?" I asked.

Aubrey closed his eyes.

"Aubs," I stated.

He opened them. "Sorry?"

"Don't pass out on me yet."

"It's my nap time."

"What was he selling?" I tried again.

"Oh, Seb, it was years ago. I think maybe it was an old pistol and a samurai sword." Aubrey nodded to himself. "Yeah, that sounds right. But I'll text you my old manager's contact information. He kept good records and reported stolen items. And if your boyfriend wants to talk to Matt… have him call the New York office and ask for Special Agent Jun Tanaka. That's his partner. Jun will put him through to Matt. I don't want Matt hearing my name at all, okay?"

"Okay, thanks."

"I have to go," Aubrey murmured, looking suddenly

exhausted. "Nap. I'll text you in about fifteen minutes." He waved briefly before the video call ended.

Max sighed. "Aubrey's so cute. I just want to pet his head and feed him cookies. Is that weird?"

I glanced sideways at Max. "Yeah, a little." I held up the picture of Richard. "If the weapons he tried to sell to an antique shop and legit pawn shop fell through, I wonder if he'd try someplace less savory?"

"But then what?" Max asked. "Sounds like a dead end."

"Unless Aubrey's old manager has an idea of where to go with hot items you need to unload fast."

Max frowned when I looked at him. "So why is Calvin letting you poke around? This doesn't have anything to do with that Roger guy I looked up for you on Facebook, right?"

"No, totally different situation."

Max reached out and nudged my arm roughly. "And?"

"A security guard at the Met was murdered. This guy—Richard."

"Holy fuck."

"Yeah. The person behind the bricks and notes—they're offing suspects from Calvin's cold cases and then making me prove the victim was guilty of murder themselves."

Max scrunched his face up, looking horrified. "This is like—like some fucked-up horror movie or something."

"Let's save that description for when I'm eventually kidnapped and forced to chew off my own hand to escape."

"Don't joke, Seb." Max ran a shaky hand through his hair. "So… who did Richard kill?"

"Cal and I think it was an old museum employee from several years ago."

"How do we prove it?"

I looked up at Max curiously. "We?" I echoed.

"If you think I'm letting you run off by yourself, you're out of your mind."

"I'm not supposed to go anywhere," I pointed out.

Max snorted. "As if you hadn't planned on heading out to wherever Aubrey tells you after he wakes up from his beauty sleep."

"I'm not letting you come. It's dangerous."

"Calvin gave me permission to disobey you. Got a problem with me tagging along, you take it up with Ginger Cop." He grinned widely.

"You're a pain."

"Now you know how we all feel about you."

Aubrey was back in the land of the living about fifteen minutes after his necessary nap. His text message was the address of his old job here in New York, the name of his boss, and a string of emoji I didn't understand. Max was reading the text out loud as I lowered the gate on the front of the Emporium.

"Then there's a kissy face, the face wearing sunglasses, a thumbs up, and a snail."

"Does all of that together mean something?"

"No. I think he's just messing with you."

"Jerk," I muttered.

After the gate was down, Max handed me back my phone, and we turned around, nearly bumping into Beth from next door. She put her hands on her hips and stood before us looking mighty displeased.

"Howdy," Max said.

"You boys going somewhere? It's the middle of the

day."

"I wasn't really open," I answered, pushing my sunglasses up.

"Calvin warned me you might try to sneak off," she said.

"He what?" I protested.

"Oh, he's good," Max said.

"I was told to call him if you went somewhere on your own." Beth raised an eyebrow. "So should I?"

"Absolutely not," I said firmly.

"He seemed pretty adamant about it."

"Calvin is also adamant about toasted bagels and the Mets," I replied.

Beth held her hands up. "The *Mets*?"

"Beth," I continued. "Just pretend you never saw us leave, okay?"

"I don't know, Sebby," she said slowly. "Are you going to get into trouble? Get hurt? Give that handsome man of yours a heart condition?"

"Maybe a little, hopefully not, and probably sooner or later," I answered.

"Smart," she said with a vicious old lady glare.

"You can reprimand me later, I promise," I said, motioning Max to follow me to the curb. "If anyone comes by looking—you never saw me, okay?"

"Sebastian Snow, are you out of your goddamn mind?"

I nodded and raised my hand up to hail a cab. "Just about."

Max and I climbed into the first taxi to stop, and I gave the driver the Midtown address before calling Calvin.

"So?" he asked upon answering.

"Hello to you too. I talked to my friend Aubrey

Grant. He used to work at a pawnshop here in the city. He recognized Richard as a guy who had been banned from the store after trying to sell items his boss suspected were stolen."

"Name and phone number?"

"Er—I'm waiting to get that from Aubrey," I lied. "He's narcoleptic and needed a nap."

"Seb."

"I would not make that up. I swear. He really is."

Calvin was quiet for a beat. "Anything else?"

"He used to date a special agent who was once on the Art Crime Team," I supplied. "He wasn't sure about any details regarding the investigation of artifacts that turned up missing after Earl was killed, but he said if you needed to get in touch with his ex, to call the New York office and ask for his partner, Jun Tanaka. He asked to keep his name out of it. Bad blood."

The driver kept glancing in the rearview mirror at me.

"All right. Thank you for this."

"What about you?"

"What about me?" Calvin asked.

"Got anything to share?"

"No."

"Filthy liar," I stated.

"Are you still at the Emporium?"

"Ah, yes. Max is right here."

"Hi, Calvin," Max called obediently.

"Earl… his bag was never recovered. By all accounts he religiously carried it, but it was never found at the museum, his home, anywhere. I believe there's still at least one or two missing artifacts, which I hope to confirm with the FBI, but I suspect them to be in his bag. Wherever that is.”

“Maybe Richard’s been holding on to it all these years. Maybe whatever the item is, it’s been too hot to sell, so he’s had to wait,” I supplied.

“You’re on the same wavelength as me,” Calvin quietly admitted. “I’m in the process of getting some officers over to his apartment.”

Max nudged my shoulder as the taxi pulled to a stop on the side of the road. He pulled some cash out of his wallet and reached through the window to pay the driver.

“I’ll let you go,” I quickly said.

“Be safe,” Calvin said before hanging up.

Max and I got out of the cab, and it made a sharp turn to once again get lost in the sea of traffic. I looked at the storefront we’d been dropped off in front of. The sign and front window to Gold Guys were hidden amongst temporary scaffolding. Hammering and general construction noise echoed from overhead, mixing with the honking of horns in Midtown traffic, chattering groups of tourists, and one guy at the corner screaming about the world ending this coming Tuesday.

Ah, the music of New York.

“What did Calvin say?” Max asked as he led the way to the door, then waited outside of it for me.

“He’s got officers heading over to Richard’s. Apparently the guy who was murdered, his bag went missing, which may still have some of the stolen items inside. I guess it’s a pretty clear-cut case if the bag is found in Richard’s home.”

“Does it count if you didn’t uncover it, though?” Max asked. “You said this freak is making *you* solve the cases.”

I hesitated. *Did* it count?

“You didn’t give Calvin the address to this place.”

"No. It'd be unfortunate if he found us here."

"You mean, you don't want him to get information before you," Max corrected.

"What can I say, I hate sharing." I opened the front door and stepped inside.

The pawnshop was brightly lit with overhead fluorescent lights, casting a strange glow on items hanging on the walls. I had to look away and focus on the floor instead.

Max whistled from behind me as he walked in. "Cool place."

"Is it? I can't see."

"Oh shit. What can I do to help?"

I shook my head and held a hand up to shield the top of my sunglasses as I stepped toward a glass display that had a man and woman organizing what I guessed was fine jewelry.

"Hey," the man said. He was a big, meaty-looking guy, with close-cropped hair. "Welcome to Gold Guys." He reached out and shook my hand. "How can I help you?"

"I'm looking for Gerald Topper," I said.

"Found him," Gerald replied, pointing at himself. He wore big rings on his hands, like those football championship ones. "And you are?"

"Sebastian Snow. I own Snow's Emporium in the East Village."

"Yeah," he said with a sort of friendly smile. "I know the place. It's been about a year or two since I've been there, but it's a nice shop."

"Oh, thank you. I'm actually here because Aubrey Grant gave me your name."

"Aubs, huh? I remember him. What's he up to these days?"

"Managing a historical home in the Keys."

"That lucky SOB."

I smiled. "I hope I'm not interrupting anything important?"

Gerald looked at the woman, and she shrugged and shook her head. "Nah. What's up? Aubs isn't in trouble, is he?"

"No, no. Nothing like that." I reached into my coat to take out the copy of Richard's ID. "He said I should talk to you about this guy."

I glanced at Max as Gerald took the picture. He gave me an excited grin.

"You're not a cop, though," Gerald stated.

I quickly looked back at him. "No."

"You watch a lot of *CSI: Miami*?"

"Aviators don't suit me, do they?"

Gerald laughed from his belly.

"I have a light sensitivity."

He nodded and didn't question me further. "Yeah, I know this guy—I never forget a face. But his name isn't Richard Newell."

"What do you mean?"

"Hold tight." Gerald left the counter and disappeared around the corner.

"This guy steal from your shop?" the woman asked, tapping the picture.

"Not exactly. But he's definitely put himself on the cops' radar."

She scoffed. "Don't expect them to do much."

"I've got an in with a particularly good cop." She didn't seem impressed by my assurance, and I found that it made me rather defensive of Calvin's reputation. He was a good—no—a great cop, damn it. If she rolled her eyes at me, we were going to have words.

Luckily Gerald came back before I had to puff out my chest. "Here we are. He got banned from my store about four years ago for trying to off-load some stolen weapons. Took off before I could get the cops involved." Gerald put an old piece of paper down on the glass countertop, the image of a faded driver's license in the middle.

"Aubrey said it was a pistol and sword," I said, pulling out my magnifying lens and leaning over the case to study the picture.

"Yeah, sounds right," he agreed.

"And this says his name is Mark Lewis," I stated before looking up at Gerald. "Do you have any idea where he might get away with selling high-value goods like that?"

Gerald crossed his huge arms over his barrel chest. "Parker's Pawn on Ninth and Fifty-First."

"That easy?" I asked.

"I've been running this shop for over twenty years, kid. I know who follows the law and who deals with dirty customers. I'm sure it's the same for you in your world."

"I guess you're right."

He laughed. "Damn true. But if you plan on going over to Parker's, you be careful. Just because he's older than sin doesn't mean he's gonna be a granddaddy to you. His son does the questionable work these days. Ben Parker's his name."

Consider me aptly warned.

I raised the paper up. "Could I have a copy?"

"Well… if Mark or Richard or whoever he is, is bothering you, you ought to—"

"He's dead," I clarified. "But I still would like a copy."

"Wow!" Max shouted as we were on the sidewalks of Midtown again, making toward Ninth Avenue. "That was so cool. You're like a totally different guy when you go sneaking around."

"Am I?"

"Hell yeah. I can see why you like this—it's kind of exciting. I take back all the crap I gave you."

"Don't get used to it."

"I won't, I won't," Max promised. "Mostly since you're not paying me to be Assistant Sleuth, right?"

"Right."

"Why did you want a copy of his old license?"

"He had a different address listed," I answered.

"So? Maybe he moved."

"Maybe. But most people don't change their full name when they move a few zip codes." I took the picture Gerald supplied me with and handed it to Max. "I might have to go check out his apartment building."

"What good will that do? It's not like he's going to come home."

"Well… no," I muttered. "But if I could somehow confirm he still occupied both apartments, it would certainly aid in Calvin's search for the missing bag." I glanced up at Max by my side. "Besides, if anything, it does make Dick-Mark seem pretty suspicious. The whole point of this insane game is simply to prove he was guilty of something during life. That seems to be all our joyful maniac wants."

"Hey, Seb?" Max stopped walking.

I turned around to look at him. "What is it?"

"I know this address."

"What?"

Max tapped the paper. "This Mark Lewis address in

Brooklyn. My buddy lives here. Same building."

"Max, don't fuck with me."

"No, I'm not kidding." Max took out his phone and snapped a picture. "Give me a second and I'll ask him if he knows the guy. He's friendly with most of his neighbors." Max handed the photo back to me and typed a quick text to his friend.

We stood between Eighth and Ninth Avenue. A cold wind ripped down the street, warm air rose from the subway grates, and the stench of piss seemed to permeate the entire block.

Max made an *ah-ha!* sound when his phone pinged. "He says, 'That guy lives on the second floor. But his name is Todd, not Mark.'"

Dick-Mark-Todd was most definitely anything but innocent.

CHAPTER THIRTEEN

"We need a plan."

"We don't need a plan."

"Every movie with spies has a plan, Seb."

"We're not in a fucking movie, Max."

"We're still spies!"

"Oh God."

"We can't just go in there asking about Mar—Todd—*the guy*. It's way too suspicious," Max said.

"That's why I alone will be asking."

"If you go in without me, I'm calling Calvin."

I swore and glanced back at Parker's Pawn. From what I could see, it looked cramped and crowded inside. The glass door had a decade's worth of old stickers and flyers taped to it. A guy stood outside the door, drinking from a paper bag. "Go inside. I'll follow."

"When you leave, I'll stick around for another minute," Max said.

"Why?"

"If they think you're suspicious or talk about you, I might be able to hear them."

Huh. Okay, that was kind of smart.

"Be careful," I said firmly.

Max smacked my shoulder in a friendly manner before walking to the front door and stepping into the shop. I waited a few minutes, just out of view. I didn't expect the owners to be forthcoming with information about a patron who sold them expensive, stolen antiques, but hell, anything would be beneficial to our search.

The smell of stale cigarette smoke assaulted my nostrils as I stepped into the shop. No one around was smoking, so it had likely leeched into the walls over the years. There were some cheap heart streamers hanging haphazardly around the register. Nothing said true love like a shop full of art thieves.

Max was standing farther in the room, talking to a guy around my age about a guitar hanging on the wall behind the counter barrier. He didn't glance my direction at all, and I had to hand it to the kid: he was really getting into this sneaking around stuff.

An old man—Parker Senior, I presumed—glanced up from his crossword puzzle behind the counter. He narrowed his eyes and sniffed. "What do you want?"

What customer service.

"Just had a quick question, sir," I said, moving to the counter. "A while back, I was trying to do business with a fellow named Mark. I had a buyer lined up for a nice samurai sword he was looking to part with, but it fell through at the last minute."

Parker Senior sniffed again and stared expectantly.

"Anyway, I was wondering if you might have known the guy's family or friends?"

"Mark who?" Parker asked.

"Lewis, I think was his name."

"Don't know a Mark Lewis. And don't know a Mark Lewis's family."

I bit my cheek to keep myself from frowning. It was hard to tell if Parker was being honest or being an asshole. I glanced to my left and noticed the younger man—perhaps Ben Parker—was staring at us and now ignoring Max. "A shame," I replied.

"Why's that?"

"Heard he died today. Wanted to give my condolences."

I dared one more look to my left, and sure enough, Ben Parker seemed very concerned at the news.

"Shit happens," Parker Senior replied. "Then you die."

"That's a bleak outlook."

He sniffed a final time and looked back down at his puzzle. I guess once you hit nine thousand years old, you've got exactly no fucks left to give. But Ben seemed to have plenty to spare, what with eventually taking over his dad's shop, I imagined. The news that one of his frequent flyers with high-quality goods would no longer be supplying a hefty lining for his wallet had to come as a shock.

"Well, thanks for your time," I said, and Parker ignored me in response.

I walked back out of the shop, crossed the street, and waited around the corner of a bodega for Max. He came out close to ten minutes later, when I was beginning to legit worry and considered running back in for him.

"*Max*," I hissed, waving him over.

He hurried toward me, letting out a breath. "That was close. I was haggling for the guitar and offered way more money than I actually have, but he didn't budge on the price." He laughed and put his hands on his hips. "Debt averted."

"You went to college," I reminded.

"*Further* debt averted!"

I rolled my eyes. "Did anything happen after I left?"

"Not exactly. But that guy was pretty chill before you entered. After, he was in a rush to make me buy or get out. Definitely acting a little weird." He glanced over his shoulder at the pawnshop before turning back to me. "What's the plan now, boss?"

"He got awfully concerned the minute I said Dick-Mark was dead. I think I should go to Brooklyn."

"We."

"You've done enough, Max."

He waved his finger in my face. "I've got Calvin on speed dial."

"What? I don't even have him on speed dial. Why are you speed- dialing my boyfriend?"

"That's for me to know and you to find out."

I shook my head and rubbed my temple. "Jesus Christ on a crutch. Now I know how Calvin feels when I tag along."

I never went to Brooklyn.

I had no reason to go to Brooklyn.

I hated Brooklyn.

Okay, I didn't hate it. But I did hate the subway. And I hated having to ride the subway to Brooklyn to hunt down stolen museum pieces from a guy found floating dead in a pool full of pennies and candy wrappers, who was responsible for brutally murdering another guy four years ago. Even if said other guy also stole priceless artifacts and probably wasn't all that nice himself.

Add to the fact that it was Saturday and trains had alternate schedules, weren't running due to maintenance and repairs, and just seemed hell-bent on fucking the general population, I really didn't like having to go to Brooklyn.

But I digress.

"Maybe you could move out here," Max said, sitting beside me on the train as we rumbled over the Williamsburg Bridge. "It's nice."

"No."

"Manhattan spoils you."

"I like being spoiled."

"You could get a cheaper place in Brooklyn."

"Yeah, maybe if I lived at Coney Island."

"What about getting a place out here with Calvin?" Max tried.

I pushed my sunglasses up on my nose and looked at him briefly. "We aren't moving in together."

"No?"

"Way too soon for that."

"I guess. Plan ahead, though."

"What do you mean?"

"You don't want to get a tiny place and six months later have to pack up and move again because *then* you want to live together. Find a decent-sized place and be ready for the next step toward domestic bliss."

"Thanks for that, Dr. Phil."

Max scoffed and shoved me. "I'm trying to help you save money in the long run."

"What stop are we?" I asked, ignoring Max's somewhat valid point.

"Myrtle Avenue."

The J train bumped along the overhead tracks and eventually rolled to a stop at our station. Max knew the neighborhood better than I did, so I followed as he led the way down from the platform. As we walked down the subway stairs, the train rattled overhead, momentarily drowning out the incessant honking of a car alarm, laughing kids on bikes, and two drunk guys arguing outside of a bodega that looked to be the sole shop in the neighborhood advertising both Mexican and Russian products.

"This way," Max said, crossing the street in between oncoming cars. "I think this address isn't all that far from the one he lists under Richard."

"At least he considered convenience for his multiple lives." I grumbled.

The sun had already begun setting for the evening as we rolled into Brooklyn, so by the time we reached the apartment about fifteen minutes away, it was nearly night. Max opened the gate to a relatively new building, strolled across the front walk, and hit the intercom.

"Yo," a crackly voice said.

"Hey, man. It's Max. Can you buzz me in?"

"Sure."

The lock on the door was released, and Max tugged it open and held it for me to follow.

The first door past the mailboxes opened and a guy about Max's age poked his head out. "What's up?"

"Long story. This is my boss, Sebastian Snow," he said, pointing at me. "Seb, my buddy Jeff from college."

"Pleasure," I answered briskly.

"I like your shades," Jeff said, nodding at me. "You look like a secret agent."

I sighed. I needed to get new sunglasses.

Max nudged Jeff's shoulder lightly. "You said your neighbor Todd lived on the second floor, right?"

"Yeah. Uh—2C, I think. Why are you asking about him?"

"Don't worry about it." I moved around Max and down the hall toward the staircase.

"I'll be back," Max said to Jeff before rushing behind me. "Should we call the cops first?" he asked, lowering his voice as we started up the stairs.

"No," I whispered.

I had a bad feeling crawling up from my gut. The hairs on the back of my neck stood on end, and I slowed to a creep as we reached the top of the first flight of stairs and turned to continue up the next set to the second floor. Logic told me to chill out because good old what's-his-name was super dead and there wasn't any danger in approaching his apartment. But my instincts warned otherwise, and they'd kept me alive this long.

I held a hand out behind me, stopping Max where he was, when I heard a muffled curse from the landing. I glanced back at him and motioned him to stay, to which he obediently nodded. I took a shaky breath and finished up the last steps in time to see someone crouched in front of the last door down the hall, sticking something in the lock and trying to break it open. The tool—maybe a screwdriver or something similar—finally made a loud noise and the door popped open.

"Hey!" I shouted.

The guy jerked his head up.

Ben Parker.

I'll be damned. I was right about something important being hidden here.

"Thief!" I called loudly, hoping someone in one of the other two apartments was home and would bear witness. "Don't move!"

Not that I thought he would listen.

Ben scrambled to his feet, looking once or twice at the open door, as if contemplating whether it was worth it, but then made directly for me and the staircase. I held up my hands to stop him and pushed hard when we made contact. But Ben was surprisingly more well-built than I gave him credit for, and he easily shoved me into the wall and hurled himself down the stairs.

I didn't stop to acknowledge the pain in my shoulder; I turned to go after Ben. Max was shouting down the stairs for him to stop before I skidded and stumbled by him. I jumped off the last few stairs and caught myself on the far wall before turning the corner and running to the front door. Jeff had come back out of his apartment, likely hearing our shouting, but was quick to move out of the way when Ben ran by and I followed right behind him.

Ben threw open the front door to the building, and I lunged after, the night a welcome relief for my eyes. We reached the sidewalk, and he took off in the direction of the subway. Even though he was obviously fit, he was bigger— and slower. I couldn't run like Calvin did, but when push came to shove, I found one more burst of energy and propelled myself forward. I shouted and grabbed the back of Ben's jacket, sending us both crashing to the pavement. A jolt of pain went from my tailbone all the way up, and I hissed while stars danced in front of my eyes.

"You nosey son of a fuck!" Ben grabbed the front of my coat and pulled me up. I barely had time to acknowledge the size of his fist before it met my face and I was knocked back against the sidewalk.

Ben hoisted me up again, but before I was able to take another pounding….

"Let him go!" Max shouted.

And then Ben was sprayed in cold foam from a fire extinguisher. I let myself drop back to avoid being hit, and Ben scrambled off me in a rush. He was coughing and trying to run again. I spit some blood from my mouth and got up, adrenaline pumping through my veins as I took off after him once more.

Ben looked over his shoulder and swore before dodging between some parked cars and crossing the street. A car honked and tires screeched. Ben hit the hood of the car and went flying through the air. I had gained too much momentum to stop in time and hit the side of the car as it came to a sudden halt.

Max was calling my name. The driver was shouting a string of obscenities. And from where I lay in the road, staring at the sky, it started to rain.

Max borrowed Jeff's umbrella, the two of us sitting on the curb as police lights flashed around us and brightened the neighborhood.

"I think I'm done being a detective with you," Max said thoughtfully. "That got way too real."

"Hmm. Where did the fire extinguisher come from?"

"It was strapped to the wall in the stairwell."

"Fast thinking."

"Yeah."

I held my hand out and Max shook it.

"Are we in trouble?" he asked next.

"No. Ah—not you, anyway."

Paramedics were wheeling Ben toward the parked ambulance, with Quinn following at his side.

I patted Max's arm. "Stay here." I stood and walked into the rain, joining her and Ben. "Guess you can't fly all that well," I said to him.

"Fuck you, asswipe."

"Classy." I took a step closer. "Who put you up to this? Who threatened you to make sure Richard was at the Temple of Dendur yesterday?"

"*What?*"

"Who threatened you?" I barked. "A big fat guy? Do you know a man named Luther North?"

"What the fuck are you on?" Ben retorted.

"Was it someone claiming to be a cop?"

His expression immediately faltered.

Oh God.

"A cop?" I asked again.

"I—"

"Did you meet him? Did you see his face? Why did you help him?" I was practically shouting.

Quinn put a firm hand on my arm and started to pull me away.

"I only ever saw him one time," Ben argued. "Then he just texted me. Said he'd throw me in jail if I didn't tell Mark—*Richard*—someone wanted to meet him at the exhibit before his shift ended."

Quinn's hold on me loosened slightly.

"And?" I prodded.

"And he said I could get back at you if I helped."

"Me? You don't even know me."

"*The fuck I don't.* I know you run that posh antique shop. You turned down purchases from my contacts. You want *papers* and your asking prices raise the market value."

"Oh, screw you! At least I'm a legitimate operation."

"Sebastian," Quinn warned, tugging me back when I took a step forward.

"I know you worked with that cranky old Rodriguez,

and *that* asshole sent the cops after me and my dad half a dozen times." Ben turned his head and spit at my feet.

"Who was the cop?" I asked, because if I didn't focus, I was going to beat his face like he had mine.

"Up yours."

"Who was the cop?" I asked again, louder. "How do you know he was legit?"

"He showed me his fucking badge, man!"

"What was his name?"

"You think he'd tell me his name?" Ben asked before laughing.

"What did he look like?"

"He looked just like a fucking cop."

I lunged to throttle that stupid bastard, but Quinn grabbed me and pushed me away. "Describe him!"

And surprisingly, even though he had paramedics and a cop to protect him from me, Ben looked a little freaked. "Tall. Brown hair. I don't know—I only saw him once."

I shoved away from Quinn, grabbed my phone, and opened the photo album. I had to scroll back in the history awhile, but I was suddenly glad I hadn't gotten around to deleting old pictures. I brought up a photo of Neil and turned the screen to Ben. "Was this him?"

"I don't know."

"*Was it?*"

"I guess so. It looks like him!" Ben cried out.

"Get him out of here," Quinn ordered, motioning for the paramedics to take Ben to the awaiting ambulance.

Jesus Christ.

Rain splattered the screen of my phone, distorting Neil's face. This couldn't be happening.

"Get out of the road," Quinn said as she opened her

umbrella and nudged me back to the sidewalk.

I walked in a daze, stuffing my phone back into my coat.

Two different people, one who knew me and one who knew of me, both claimed a cop threatened to jail them if they didn't help ensure the victims show up at a museum in order to be killed. Both said they only met him once, then received text messages afterward. All of the clues and threats for and against me were personal. Someone who had a good understanding of my habits and inner circle.

And only one person in my life had reason to hate me.

Neil did. I believed that now—that he truly hated me for our breakup.

But was he so angry, so beside himself, *over me*, that he snapped? I wanted to say it was absolutely, without a doubt, the most convoluted bullshit I'd ever heard. Except when someone goes missing or suffers a tragic fate, spouses or partners are often the first to be questioned or even suspected.

Love can be our own worst enemy. If you're not strong enough to wield it, you could succumb to its darker side: hatred and jealousy.

I realized belatedly that an umbrella had ended up over my head, and when I looked up, Calvin was standing in front of me.

"Hi, baby," he said quietly.

"I know you're angry," I answered.

He only nodded.

"I deserved the split lip and bruised ass."

Calvin reached out and lifted my chin with a gentle touch to inspect where Ben had punched me.

"Was there anything in the apartment?"

Calvin let go of my face and looked between myself

and Quinn. "We took a quick look inside. Found a bag matching the description of Earl's that was never recovered from the scene. There was a piece of china inside, as well as an old pistol. I'll call the FBI, but I'm sure they'll match the last items stolen from the Met."

"So did we prove Richard guilty?"

"Forensics will need to fingerprint everything," Calvin answered. "But… it's looking pretty solid, yeah."

Forensics. Neil.

"Cal? About that—"

"Hey, Seb," Max said as he wandered over to us. "Can I go home?" He offered a lopsided grin. "And maybe have tomorrow off?"

"Sure thing," I said with a weary laugh.

"I'll get him home," Quinn offered.

Max said his good-byes, and Quinn ushered him away from the scene to drive him herself. Police continued to fill the block, going in and out of the building and stopping to talk with Calvin, who still stood at my side. I even caught Officer Brigg standing at the apartment building's front door. She noticed me and tipped her hat in my direction.

I fell asleep in Calvin's car while I waited for him to finish at the scene. I didn't wake until the engine started and his warm, strong hand rested briefly on my thigh.

"Hey," I mumbled, pulling my sunglasses off and rubbing my eye carefully to fix a contact. "I didn't mean to fall asleep."

"It's all right," he whispered. "I'll wake you when we're in the city again."

Calvin turned the radio on to a low setting that barely qualified as white noise, and pulled onto the road. He didn't seem to be in the mood for talk, so I remained quiet. I leaned my head against the passenger window, watching the streetlights pass by, their reflections bouncing off the windshield and raindrops. The sound of the windshield wipers lulled me back to sleep, my body unable to fight the urge after all of the adrenaline I'd spent chasing Ben.

I woke again after reaching Manhattan. We were sitting in traffic, waiting for the light to change. Calvin had his elbow against the door, resting his chin on his fist, while his other hand tapped the wheel absently. I reached out and put my hand on his and was grateful when he turned his palm up and briefly threaded our fingers together.

Calvin turned and looked at me. "I'm sorry. I should have kept you out of this."

"It's no one's fault but my own." I held his hand tighter. "I knew what I was doing."

He returned the squeeze. "It's my job to protect you. And you put up a hell of a fight when I try to do so, no matter what."

I nodded. "I know. And no matter how many times I've told myself to drop this, to let it go and just be a law-abiding citizen, something pulls me back in."

Calvin let go of my hand when the light changed and traffic began to move.

"I'm good at solving mysteries."

"Yes, you are."

I looked at him.

Calvin glanced sideways at me. "I never denied that."

I felt myself smile.

"I love you, Sebastian. I want you far away from these messes because—you shouldn't have to be witness to such monstrous behavior. And maybe that comes from… the part of me that… needs help. I don't want you to ever wake in a cold sweat from nightmares."

Traffic stopped again.

Calvin looked at me. "But… you're so smart. And I do see the appeal in figuring these puzzles out, especially when they directly involve you. Should our positions be reversed, maybe you'd be constantly yelling at me to butt out."

"I can't tell if you're happy or upset with me," I said honestly.

"Both. I'm just worried," he said. "All I want you to promise me is, when it comes to murder and mystery, just call and let me know what you plan on getting yourself into."

I smiled again and leaned over in my seat, meeting Calvin halfway and kissing him. "I promise."

The traffic was stop-and-go the rest of the way to his apartment. Calvin found a parking spot about a block away, and he held an umbrella over us both, arm around my shoulders, as we walked to his building. Everything seemed almost *normal*, until we reached his apartment door inside, which was slightly ajar.

Calvin immediately pushed me behind him, set his umbrella aside, and pulled out his pistol. He took a readied stance and pushed open the door to the dark studio, reaching in to flick on the wall switch.

My heart was hammering loud in my ears, and I strained to look around Calvin and inside his apartment. "Cal?"

He didn't respond and instead took a few steps inside. He immediately disappeared around the left corner, and I could hear him checking the bathroom. Calvin moved back into view, checking his closet and getting down to look under the bed last. Standing, he paused midway in holstering his weapon while staring at his pillow.

"Cal?" I said again.

"Come here," he said in a low tone.

I went inside, honestly feeling a little sick from the second rush of adrenaline. "What is it?" I joined his side to see what he was staring at.

A pamphlet.

An old one.

Maybe around thirty pages. The cover page listed it as twelve cents to purchase.

Barnum's American Museum illustrated.

The quality was impeccable. Even without taking the time to look through it, I'd have to say the condition was near fine. I took a step toward the bed and snatched a folded note beside the book before Calvin could stop me.

Congratulations!

Dead fish can't swim.

"There's no address," I said, turning the paper over to double check. "How do I know where to go?" I gave it to Calvin and reached for the pamphlet.

"No," Calvin said firmly, grabbing my hand. "And we're not staying here. Get some things, put them in a bag."

"What? Where are we going?"

"A hotel."

Not that a night together in a hotel didn't have its perks. But if I wanted a king-sized bed, mints on the pillows, and sex in the sheets, I'd have preferred it to be tomorrow on Valentine's Day, after our disgustingly romantic date that Calvin still didn't know I wanted.

I'd have preferred to keep psycho killers and P.T. Barnum out of it.

CHAPTER FOURTEEN

Calvin made good money.

It was fairly obvious based on the hotel suite in Midtown that he got us.

Not a room—a *suite*.

I whistled as he shut the door. "Was all this necessary?"

"Yes."

I laughed and shook my head. "If you insist." I dropped my haphazardly packed bag onto the couch and then kicked off my shoes. I changed into my regular glasses and went across the room to open the fridge. "Full bar. We can get drunk and make some bad decisions later."

"I have to make some calls." Calvin set aside his coat and loosened his tie. "Will you be all right?"

I nodded. "Of course." I went over to him and slid my hands from his flanks down to his hips. "Hungry? I can order some room service."

"Yeah, thank you. Anything is fine." Calvin kissed me gently before he excused himself and went into the bedroom.

I sat at the table and flipped open a binder to look through the dinner options. Calvin's deep, sexy voice was muffled by the wall, but in the end, I had to turn on the television to drown him out completely, lest I be tempted to eavesdrop. He ended up being on the phone for an entire episode of some house-renovating show.

When room service arrived, I answered the door and tipped the guy before taking our meals to the table. I went to the bedroom door and knocked lightly, peeking inside in time to hear Calvin thank and address someone as Special Agent.

My boyfriend's cooler than anyone else's because he has the FBI in his contact list.

"Seb?" Calvin asked as he lowered the phone from his ear.

"Dinner's here."

"Good timing," he said, following me out.

I pointed to the plates. "Steak or mac and cheese?"

Calvin raised an eyebrow.

"It's fancy mac and cheese," I clarified.

Calvin looked at the steak.

I rolled my eyes and pushed him to the left chair. "Go nuts."

"Are you sure you don't want it?" Calvin asked, taking a seat.

"Don't worry. I really ordered it for you," I insisted. "I'd make some lewd comment about being sure to get my fill of protein later, but I'm tired. Did you finish with your calls?"

Calvin nodded as he started going at the steak. "Finished," he agreed between bites.

"Any important revelations?"

He looked up. "Spoke with Special Agent Tanaka at the FBI, per your friend's suggestion. He put me through to Special Agent Matt O'Sullivan, who was on the original case four years ago. He confirmed the china and pistol we found tonight are indeed the two items reported as stolen by the Met the same time Earl was murdered."

"I'll be damned."

Calvin nodded.

"And since the Barnum guidebook was at your place, I guess we solved it in the killer's eyes too."

"Seems as much," Calvin muttered around another mouthful.

"What do we do about that? Not that this hotel isn't swanky as fuck. I rather like it, but we can't live here."

"I've informed my sergeant," Calvin said.

"About… just the book?" I asked hesitantly.

But I knew that wouldn't be the case. Because Calvin was a good cop, and he'd have already put it in on record that I was the one being harassed. The book had been left at his place because the killer knew it was home to me as well.

"I told him the truth—mostly," Calvin said as he looked up from his plate. "I told him you and your employee were visiting his friend and stumbled upon Ben Parker trying to break into an apartment. You both took it upon yourselves to try to keep him at bay until the cops arrived. When it became clear who lived there, I was called. After I finished, I brought you back to my place, because we've been dating for over a month, and we found the book."

I swallowed. "Well, it's basically true."

"More or less," Calvin said with a frown.

"Did he get pissed at you?"

"Yes."

"Are you going—" I didn't want to finish the thought.

"To lose my job?" Calvin asked for me. "No. He just chewed my ass out and threatened to suspend me."

"Calvin!"

"He won't, baby."

"Jesus Christ, this is all my fault." I dropped my fork and shoved the cheesy mess away. "Can I—should I talk to him? I'll tell him—"

Calvin shook his head. "No. Please don't, okay? I've gotten the reaming I deserved, because I shouldn't have been involved with this."

"But we were dating before this happened."

"I've been too personally invested."

"How can you be so calm about this?"

"My sergeant is a decent guy. He's made his point, and I'll be on a short leash for a bit, but everything will work itself out."

I took my glasses off and scrubbed my face hard with my hands. "I'm an awful boyfriend," I mumbled into my palms.

"Don't be silly."

I looked up at Calvin's blurry figure. "How could you possibly not agree after all this? After getting in trouble with your boss?"

Calvin let out a quiet sigh and pushed his plate aside. He stood, and I thought maybe he was going to walk away, but instead he crouched down in front of me and took my hands into his. "Sebastian. I've never had anyone fight like you do to love me. I can't... begin to explain what it feels like... to be so broken inside that happiness with another man seems impossible. And then you come barging in, forcing me to rethink everything I had convinced myself of."

I squeezed Calvin's hands. No matter what he thought of himself, there was no one I knew who was stronger or braver than he was. Not in a moment like this.

"But even if you do stupid things—and, sweetheart, you are the king of bad ideas—you haven't given up on me, and maybe… that isn't…."

"*Stupid?*" I supplied quietly.

Calvin's mouth worked into not quite a smile, but not quite a frown. "Yeah." He looked down at our hands. "It scares the hell out of me," he whispered. "To talk about this, or—or getting lost in the system if I reach out for help. It scares me to stop working as much as I do, because what if it opens a floodgate? What if I turn into a vet who can't control his anger or fear and I hurt you?"

"Calvin—"

He raised my hands up and kissed the knuckles gently. "All I mean to say is, you make me happy, Sebastian. And that to me is the sign of a damn good partner."

I pulled my hands away and moved them up to cup Calvin's face before I leaned down to kiss him. "You make me happy too." I got down from my chair to be eye level with him. "Can I tell you something lame?"

"Sure."

"If none of this crap had ruined the holiday, I was going to ask if you'd go on a really over-the-top, painfully romantic date with me."

Sitting this close, I could see Calvin slowly smile, and then he chuckled. "Why *painfully* romantic?"

"I've always wanted to do the whole dinner and flowers and stuff," I said, shrugging.

"You should have told me," Calvin said simply.

"Yeah, but I wanted you to enjoy being all gushy in love with me, not just put up with it."

"I'd like it."

I felt my face heat up. "Oh. I guess I'll keep that in mind for next year."

"There's still this year," Calvin offered.

"Valentine's Day is tomorrow. There's no way we'll find reservations at a nice restaurant, and you'll undoubtedly be busy."

"So we'll have our own little date tonight." Calvin reached over to the table and retrieved my glasses, then slid them back onto my face. "We had some nice room service."

"I should have ordered something classier," I stated glumly.

"We're in an expensive hotel."

"Were there mints on the pillows?"

Calvin glanced over his shoulder at the bedroom door. "I don't think so."

I scoffed.

"But the hand towels were folded to look like swans."

"Okay, that's kind of nice," I admitted.

Calvin laughed and leaned in to kiss my mouth. "I know you grabbed the condoms," he whispered against my lips. "Let's go in the bedroom and I'll make you scream my name."

I shivered at the invitation.

I *had* thought to grab Calvin's condoms—but I'd also thrown toothbrushes and shaving cream in the bag, so maybe it was more of an instinctive thing.

I slid my arms around Calvin's neck, kissing him back. "How about you scream mine?"

Calvin sat up on his knees, tugging me forward. "That sounds perfect," he murmured.

We both got to our feet, and I pushed Calvin backward

while yanking his tie free. "You should probably use this on me someday," I said, twisting the fabric briefly around my wrists.

"You're so fucking hot." Calvin grabbed me by the back of the head and kissed me hard.

"Ouch! Split lip."

"Sorry." He kissed the side of my mouth in an apology.

I dropped Calvin's tie and made quick work of his button-down shirt. I shoved it from his shoulders and tossed it behind me. I ran my palms firmly along his chest while looking down. Calvin was straining against his trousers, and I loved that he was this excited and turned on for what we were going to do.

"Get naked and lay on the bed," I ordered.

Calvin growled playfully in response, leaned down, and kissed and bit my neck instead.

My dick was painfully hard, aching for attention. I briefly succumbed to his ministrations, my own breathing hitching and a moan escaping my lips. "N-No," I finally said. "Play fair. Pants off and be waiting for me." I pushed Calvin into the bedroom.

I turned and sprinted across the living room, then grabbed the bag I'd tossed on the couch. My shoulder and ass still hurt from where I'd been shoved into the wall and avoided nearly being run over, but those were poor excuses to miss out on sex with a gorgeous man in a bed so big, one side would have to send me a postcard reading *Wish you were here*! I made a mess, tossing clothes and toiletries aside, before snatching the lube and cursing until I found a condom.

Ready to go, I dropped the bag, ran to the bedroom, and skidded to a stop at the sight of Calvin sprawled out across the comforter. He had one arm resting behind his head, his free hand lazily stroking his huge cock. Damn… Calvin should have needed a permit to walk around with that thing locked and loaded.

"You like this?" he asked.

"Is that a trick question?" I stepped forward, then set the items down beside Calvin's leg before I yanked my sweater and shirt off, dropping them to the floor.

Calvin gave an appreciative murmur as he watched. "Come on, sweetie. Show me the cock that's going to fuck me senseless."

"My skills aren't exactly up to par," I warned, shucking my jeans off. I climbed onto the bed once I was naked and moved up toward Calvin. "It's been, like… three years."

"You'll be fine," he said, reaching out to pull me closer.

I straddled Calvin's lap, rocking lazily against him as we kissed. We'd both memorized each other's bodies, had learned the strength and speed and motion needed to bring each other to the brink of blinding, scorching-hot bliss. Calvin's hands pressed firmly along my shoulder blades, roamed down the links of my spine, and smoothed over my ass. I leaned down to give the beautiful freckles over his neck and chest plenty of kisses. I dragged my tongue over the hollow of his throat, and Calvin's breath caught.

"Good?" I whispered.

"It's always good with you. How do you want me?"

"Always naked, at my every beck and call."

"I think Quinn may protest the sight of my balls and ass every day."

I wiggled my eyebrows. "Pretty freckled ass."

He kneaded my own in response. "Don't make me beg."

"Would you?" I asked before nibbling Calvin's

earlobe.

He let out a groan and tightened his grip on my ass. "I need your cock. I need it stretching my hole—need to feel it all day tomorrow."

"All day? I'll do my best, but I'm thinking you'll be out of luck by ten—maybe eleven."

"Shut up and fuck me," Calvin murmured.

I swallowed and nodded. "All right."

I leaned back to grab the lube and poured some on my fingers. Calvin stretched his legs apart and raised one to his chest, giving me complete access. I moved over him once again, kissing Calvin deep as I pressed my fingers in. I tried to emulate how he prepared me, tried to make it a pleasure all its own and not treat it like just a necessity. When he bucked and gasped against my lips, I found myself grinning.

"Found the on switch."

"Jesus Christ," Calvin swore. "God, more, Seb."

"Don't fill up on the appetizer."

"This isn't—*fuck*!" Calvin grabbed at me, gripping and caressing whatever he could reach.

I tried to spend another moment preparing, but the way that Calvin's breathing had become erratic and the desperate way he tugged on his own cock made me stop. "Deep breath," I said, stopping to open the condom wrapper.

"Shit. Come on. Hurry up."

I glanced back at him, grinning. "Listen to you. My big strong knight."

"You like hearing me beg?"

"I do," I admitted.

I squirted more lube and rubbed myself slick. It was now or never. Positioning myself over Calvin, I nudged the head of my cock against his opening and pushed into the ring of muscle. The tight heat was incredible. His body hugged my dick, pulling it into itself and making me lose my breath.

"You're so fucking gorgeous," Calvin murmured. He looked down between us as I thrust forward once. "Yeah… that's right."

"Is it okay?"

Calvin moaned in response, the noise he made sending a sharp thrill straight to my balls.

"Faster?"

"Faster."

I grabbed both of Calvin's hands next, sliding my fingers through his and raising his arms above his head. I held him there and started moving in earnest. The slap of my balls against his ass was hotter than I can say, and I gripped his hands painfully tight as wave after wave of pleasure threatened to rock me right out of the boat.

I could see why Calvin managed to dirty talk so well when he fucked me. When I bottomed—so to speak—it was so goddamn overwhelming, I was surprised I remembered to breathe half of the time. But on the giving end, I found myself able to think a bit more.

Not much, mind you. But enough.

And having Calvin underneath, writhing and panting and gasping for more of me… it boosted a strange sense of confidence. I wanted to please him through whatever means were necessary.

"You like having a cock up your ass?"

Calvin smiled wickedly at me. "Yeah, baby. I love your thick cock breaking me wide open."

"Want me to come inside you?"

Calvin groaned loudly in response. "I want you to come on my chest."

I let go of one of Calvin's hands and wrapped it

around his neck. "Ask sweetly." I squeezed a bit and he gasped.

"Oh yeah, God—Seb!"

"Ask for it," I ordered before pulling back and giving one hard thrust forward.

"Take my ass! Oh God. Please, make a mess on me."

I maneuvered down low and kissed Calvin's mouth. "Good boy," I whispered.

"*Fuck*. Sebastian," he moaned, then kissed me back hard.

I pressed my forehead to Calvin's and sped up my motions when I felt that telltale prickle start along my spine. I took as much pleasure as I could stand in that moment, savoring the last few thrusts into that perfect heat that slid around me like a glove, but I was ready to bust, and the thought of jacking off over Calvin's chest was driving me insane.

I pulled out, quickly tugged the condom off, and tossed it somewhere I'd later regret. I put a knee between Calvin's legs and got closer before pumping myself hard. "You're so good," I said, looking down at him.

Calvin's body was splayed out. His skin had taken on a darker shade that I knew was a flush against his usually pale complexion, his lips were swollen from kisses, and in general looking gorgeously fucked and happy about it.

"Can I touch myself?" he asked quietly.

"Not until I finish," I answered.

Calvin made a sound that was very much arousal and not frustration. He reached up and grabbed my hips, holding me above him. "Come on," he purred. "Paint my chest."

And I couldn't hold back another second. I came hard, left breathless in the aftermath. I looked down to see ropes of my own cum glistening in Calvin's chest hair, and damn if it wasn't the hottest image I'd seen in a long time.

"I need to finish," Calvin begged.

"Go ahead," I managed to say between pants.

Calvin reached down and quickly jerked himself off, coming after just a few tugs. If he could have gotten any more limp and sated-looking afterward, he managed it. "My toes curled," he finally stated.

I got down and gently kissed his lips. "That good?"

He chuckled airily. "Yes." Calvin tilted his head and smiled as he reached up to comb hair back from my forehead. "Thank you. You're absolutely perfect."

My chest tightened. Instead of making a stupid joke or sarcastic remark, I simply said, "I love you, Cal."

Calvin kissed the top of my head.

I grumbled and turned away, hugging my pillow. If he was awake, that meant it was morning, and I was having none of that right now.

"Rise and shine."

"No," I muttered.

I heard Calvin laugh as he got up from the bed. He moved around the room, steps muffled by the plush carpet. The sound of plastic crinkled, and when I opened my eyes, there was something huge, blurry, and pretty-smelling being thrust at me.

"What… the hell?" I grumbled, sitting up.

"Sorry." Calvin handed over my glasses with his other hand. "You'll need these."

I put them on and blinked the sleep from my eyes. Then I saw what Calvin had been holding in front of him: a huge bouquet of flowers. I must have looked confused.

"Happy Valentine's Day," he stated. "I realized I

don't know your favorite flower—but I remembered the first night we talked about the Andrews case together, you had a bouquet of carnations… so…." He glanced down at the flowers in his hand and shrugged lightly.

It was at least two dozen carnations, all wrapped carefully in heavy plastic to hold them in place and tied with a big bow. The shades of gray varied, so I assumed they were quite colorful.

"When did you get these?" I asked.

"This morning, while you were asleep."

I realized belatedly he was already dressed for work.

"Oh. I mean, no—I like them."

Calvin seemed, maybe a bit—nervous?

"I really do," I insisted, giving him a sleepy smile. "No one's ever bought me flowers. Duncan Andrews doesn't count."

"If you don't like carnations…."

"I do. *Like them*, I mean," I blurted out. "This was really sweet of you. You're playing into my mushy, lovey-dovey fantasies quite well."

Calvin leaned down and wrapped a hand around the back of my neck as he kissed me. "I better get going."

"So soon?"

"It's after eight."

"Wow, really?" I turned to look at the alarm clock. "I slept like the dead."

"The dead don't drool."

"Shut up. I don't drool," I said defensively.

"I beg to differ."

"You're an ass."

He laughed.

I set the flowers to my side and took Calvin's hands. "Before you go. I showed a picture to Ben Parker last night. Of Neil. Ben said he looked like the cop that… that threatened him the same way Luther was."

Calvin narrowed his eyes. "What there is against Neil right now is circumstantial at best." It was horrifying to know that Calvin and I had been thinking the same thing about Neil, and yet at the same time, a relief that I wasn't alone or insane for having these thoughts.

"I know. But… two people both gave the same story of a cop threatening jail time if they didn't comply. And Neil… is… angry. At me. I can't believe it, but—" I stopped and just shrugged.

"I understand."

"Do you have ballistics from either of the murders?"

Calvin ran his thumb over my knuckles. "Both wounds were inflicted with a service pistol. We're still waiting to see if it matches anything in the system."

"And what about the number that texted Luther and Ben?"

"The one that sent Luther messages was a prepaid phone. Probably tossed afterward. I'll have to confirm if the same number was used to reach Ben."

"You need to go collect the pamphlet from your apartment," I said next. "There has to be mention somewhere of the address regarding the next clue. There's a dead body out there waiting to be found."

Calvin didn't respond to that, instead raising my hand up and kissing it. "Do you plan on staying here today?"

"I really would like to go by the shop and at least collect my mail. In and out."

He started to speak, but his cell rang in his coat pocket. Calvin let go of my hands, retrieved his phone, and put it to his ear. "Detective Winter."

I sighed and looked around the room briefly. I

needed to find where my clothes went. Maybe I should go shopping today. Pop and I could go, and I'd forget all about the fact that Calvin would be at work, getting his ducks in a row so that he could arrest Neil. God… the thought made me feel sick.

"Copy. I'm on my way in now." Calvin hung up and glanced down at me.

"Waiting for me to ask?"

He nodded.

"What'd you find out? Bullet match?"

"No. An ID on the dead man in your apartment. Enough remains were found to do a dental comparison."

"And?"

"A cop. Officer Brian Lowry."

"A cop?" I repeated, pushing the blankets aside and getting to my feet.

Calvin tucked his phone back into his pocket.

"Why the fuck was there a dead cop in my house?"

"Good question."

"Do you know him?"

"No."

"Maybe Neil does," I mumbled while looking down at my feet.

Calvin kissed my forehead and stepped away from the bed.

"Wait, you said Lowry?" I asked, following behind him.

"Yeah."

"I know an Officer Lowry," I stated, sort of surprised. "He was one of the cops who came by when I reported the vandalism and break-in at the Emporium. Oh no—do you think his partner could be in danger?"

It was spitting snow when I reached the Emporium.

Snow or sleet or freezing rain. The city just couldn't get ahead this year.

Calvin had left the hotel pretty quickly after his phone call. I lingered for a bit, taking my time to shower and dress before heading out for the morning. Pop agreed to meet up for lunch and go shopping after. Holding my hand while picking out clothes was nothing new for him, but he willingly did it because Pop knew better than anyone the frustration I'd gone through as a kid with complete achromatopsia. It was probably the one thing that still made me self-conscious.

I'd also warned him that I wanted to try department stores again. I supposed it was kind of good timing that all my crap clothes had been torched, because I was finally starting to care about my appearance again. I'd never be a model or the boy next door, but Calvin made me feel like I was. And that sort of confidence wants a pair of jeans that fit in the ass.

I let out a breath as I retrieved my keys to bring up the Emporium's gate. The cold air clouded around my mouth.

A car door slammed on the street behind me.

"Seb!"

My heart took a diving leap into the pit of my stomach. My fingers shook and I dropped the keys. I crouched and quickly picked them up before standing and turning to see Neil striding across the street toward me.

"We need to talk," he said loudly.

"I don't think so," I answered.

"Don't give me attitude," he ordered as he stepped onto the sidewalk.

I felt myself take a step back. Fight-or-flight was

kicking in real hard. "Why are you doing this? *Why*?"

Neil narrowed his eyes and shook his head. "This is what happens when you get involved with shit over your head, Sebastian. Do you see what happens when you think you're a cop? Do you see how bad of an idea it is to date someone like Winter? You've been nearly killed how many times this week?"

"You'd know," I shouted. "Oh my God. *Holy God, Neil*. This is insane!"

"I want you back," Neil said firmly. "I'll forgive you for sleeping with Winter."

"Like hell. Are you nuts?"

"Sebastian—" Neil grabbed my arm.

"Don't touch me!" I tore away from his hold and reached into my jacket for my phone. "I'm calling the cops."

"I *am* a cop."

"You're a monster!" I screamed. I was trying to unlock my phone, but I was shaking so hard, I kept typing in the wrong fucking password.

Neil grabbed me again, yanking my arm and causing me to drop the phone. He looked down and smashed the heel of his shoe on the screen. "You keep this between us."

Neil reeked of booze. He looked angry. *Mean*. And he was scaring the hell out of me.

"Everything okay here, gentlemen?" a third voice spoke suddenly.

I jerked my head to the side in time to see Officer Brigg getting out of her cruiser. She put her hands on her belt and stared at us expectantly.

"We're fine," Neil barked.

Brigg looked to me. "Mr. Snow?"

I ripped free from Neil's painful grip. "No, we're not." I walked toward her. "Could I have a ride? I need to talk to Detective Winter," I explained, reaching into my back pocket for my wallet and handing her one of his cards.

She glanced up, looking between me and Neil a few steps away.

"Please," I whispered.

Brigg nodded. "No problem." She opened the back door of her cruiser. "Hop in."

I didn't even bother to crack some wiseass joke about needing handcuffs if I were to sit in the back, because I was too scared. Shit had gotten real with Neil. Whoever he had been when we were dating… that man was gone. I shut my eyes and leaned as far over as I could in the seat, taking deep breaths.

Brigg got back in behind the wheel and pulled onto the street. "Domestic dispute?"

I clenched my jaw and gripped my thighs.

Breathe in. Breathe out.

Brigg was singing quietly to herself, then after a moment, asked, "Detective Winter is your boyfriend?"

I opened my eyes and glanced up, catching her gaze in the rearview mirror. "How do you know that?"

"He's a highly decorated officer. Him coming out of the closet sticks in people's minds."

"Oh." I fidgeted on the uncomfortable seat. "I heard about your partner. Lowry."

She hummed in acknowledgment.

"I'm sorry."

"So am I."

Weird.

I looked back down, staring at my shoes and focusing on relaxing my balled-up hands. There was something on the floor of the cruiser. I pushed my sunglasses up and reached down to touch the grainy dust with my fingertips. I brought it up close to examine and realized with a startling sense of dread....

Brick dust.

I slowly looked toward the front seat. Brigg was watching me in the rearview mirror again. She had driven too far east and was several blocks the wrong direction from Calvin. "Brigg," I said, trying to hide the concern creeping into my voice. "You're going the wrong way."

She didn't reply.

"You're heading straight for the East River—"

River?

Dead fish can't swim.

"Taxidermy," Brigg said, as if I'd asked a question. "Taxidermy fish was the third prize." She looked back into the mirror. "But that'll be hard to award you, since even a sleuth as decent as you can't solve his own murder."

CHAPTER FIFTEEN

The one time I was more than happy to call Calvin, and I was without the means.

"You're pretty smart," Brigg continued. "I saw that in December. I heard what you'd done to help solve the Nevermore case. You're pretty crazy, aren't you?"

I tried to swallow, but my mouth was too dry. "Takes one to know one."

She seemed amused. "When I decided to do what I did, I knew I needed someone to care. Really care. You didn't disappoint."

"Do what you did?" I repeated. "You mean murder innocent people?"

"They weren't innocent," Brigg said in a low tone. "Murderers themselves."

I shook my head. "I don't get it. You organized this entire charade for what?"

"For you." Brigg smiled into the mirror. "Because I knew you'd care."

"Luther and Ben weren't murderers," I exclaimed. "Why threaten to throw them in jail if they didn't help?"

"Liars and thieves. It was only a matter of time before either of those low-lives escalated."

"Jesus fucking Christ," I swore.

So it wasn't Neil.

Oh God.

I'd nearly *ruined* his life. But the evidence against him—knowing the layout of my shop, a male cop identified by Ben, knowing about my habits, my home....

"I am a little surprised you didn't put two and two together sooner," Brigg said. "I showed up everywhere. I thought you'd notice that."

"I—I did," I managed to say. "But I thought...."

"Who did you think it was?"

"The guy I was arguing with outside my shop."

"He does look an awful lot like Lowry, doesn't he? That was sheer luck," Brigg said with a small smile. She made another turn, driving at a leisurely pace toward the East River. The snow had turned to a heavy rain, and the day had darkened considerably.

"What was the point of all this?"

"What did you think?" she countered.

"I don't.... You wanted me to prove guilt."

"Yes. The system sure as hell isn't. Murderers and rapists are let loose every day because of a shaky alibi or mishandled evidence."

"So you decided to take it upon yourself to play the judge, jury, and executioner?" I grabbed at the door handles, but I knew it was pointless. The backseat of cruisers couldn't be opened from the inside. "Why the fucking P.T. Barnum gags? The bricks, the mermaid, Jefferson... you killed your own partner!"

Brigg's smile had disappeared. "Justice is absolute. And a corrupt cop I'll proudly take out."

Oh. The. Irony.

"And what did he do to deserve being shot and dressed like a joke from Barnum's museum?"

"Took bribes."

I tried the fucking doors again, more desperately.

"My great-great-grandfather was one of the firemen who went to Barnum's museum. He had been rescuing the staff and actors inside—saved a few artifacts as well. Never knew what to do with all that junk until I met you," Brigg said in a thoughtful, almost dreamy tone. "But it's like all the stuff in your store. Right up your alley, isn't it? Kept you coming back for more."

I looked around the backseat for something, *anything*, to help me in this situation. But it was empty. A safe place to keep a handcuffed suspect. Or a sleuth you planned on sending out for a swim and not coming back with.

"Lowry helped you do all this, then?" I asked. What else could I do but keep her talking? "He met with Luther and Ben, right?"

"Sure. Once, like I'm certain they both claimed. But it was too difficult working with a man who'd rather have a few hundred bucks over helping me realize a greater good."

"I thought it was Neil," I whispered. "I was so convinced it was him...."

"I don't have to know forensics to understand how to dismantle a security alarm and get around two poorly placed cameras," Brigg pointed out.

"But knowing where I lived? Where Cal—Winter lives?"

"I followed you."

"And the bricks?"

"What about them?"

"Why Buffalo Block bricks?" I shook my head. "I never understood."

"I figured the best way to draw out your curiosity was an antique. You can really buy anything on the internet these days. Two hundred antique bricks for fifty bucks." She looked in the mirror again. "Anyway. It hooked you, didn't it? Just like Barnum hooked 'em with bricks."

"You nearly blew me up before your fucking game even started!" I screamed.

Brigg's expression got dark. "Sit back and behave, Mr. Snow." She drove a few minutes longer in silence, eventually finding a place to park alongside the East River Greenway. Brigg shut off the car, took the keys from the ignition, and turned in her seat. "Let me make it clear. Lowry made the bomb. Useless fuck. It wasn't supposed to take the building down—just be enough to start the fire and dispose of his body. At least you survived, hmm?"

I didn't want to get out of the car. If I got out, I wasn't going to make it home alive.

I knew that.

Brigg knew that.

I had to stall. I had to keep right where I was until someone came by who I could scream to for help.

But a quick glance out the window told me that wasn't likely to happen. In this bitterly cold rain and wind, right by the river? The walk was empty, even during the late morning.

Brigg opened her door and got out. She adjusted her cap and belt with an unreasonable sense of calm before opening my door. "Come on out, Mr. Snow."

I didn't move.

She sighed, removed the pistol from her side, and pointed it directly at me. "Out," she said again.

Every nerve in my body screamed at me to run as I climbed out. *Turn and bolt down the boardwalk as fast as your fucking legs can!* But I wasn't Superman. I wasn't going to outrun a bullet.

And even if I tried, Jell-O legs weren't going to get me far.

My heart was pounding so hard and fast that it was making me nauseous.

Brigg motioned with her gun to walk toward the railing that overlooked the water. "I'm glad we had this time together."

I glanced over my shoulder. "What have I done to deserve being shot?"

"Nothing."

"Then why kill me? You had it planned, right?"

"Oh yes."

"But... *why*?" I sounded desperate.

Brigg didn't speak until we reached the railing. I turned to stare at her, the wind tearing through my jacket and making me feel as if I were naked. The rain pelted my glasses and face.

She raised her pistol, pointing it at me. "I can't keep defending justice by myself. It's too much for one person. But I can't stop. I just... *can't*... not when there's so much wrong in this world." Brigg took a firing stance. "At least you helped me for a time."

"I definitely didn't help you," I said, nearly laughing because at this point, I was hysterical.

"You did, though. Others saw the victims for the filth they were." She shook her head. "But it's just too much for one person."

"You can't live with the guilt of killing, but you can't stop either? So you're shooting me to get caught. Is that right?"

"About so, yes."

Tears were welling up in my eyes. My chin quivered. "I don't want to die," I said simply. "I have a family. I can't—" The words failed to escape me.

"I'm sorry," Brigg said with a somber tone. "There's no other way. It has to be you."

A sob tore out of me. I couldn't—I couldn't leave my dad behind.

I'm supposed to bury him, not the other way around.

And Calvin.

There were countless more sunrises to wake up to with him at my side. An impossible number of smiles and laughs to share. I owed him a million and one more *I love yous*.

And so far my count was three.

"Hands on your head," Brigg said calmly.

"Please don't," I tried.

"Now."

Tears rolled down my face as I slowly put my hands on the back of my head.

"Turn around. Don't worry—it'll be quick."

I took a shaky breath and slowly turned my back to her. I looked out over the choppy, gray waters of the East River. "I love you," I whispered, hoping somehow Calvin heard me.

"*Sebastian!*"

I turned toward the left in shock. It was hard to make out the person, but I knew the voice. Neil was running from his parked car, gun in hand, and he took aim at Brigg and shot. I covered my head and crouched instinctively, looking back as she stumbled hard into a bench.

No blood, though.

She had a vest on under the winter coat.

Brigg raised her pistol and shot, and Neil's body jerked back violently and fell.

"No!" I lunged forward. I had no idea what I was doing. There had been no thought, no split-second decision. I was acting on animalistic instincts to survive.

I grabbed Brigg and threw us both to the ground, rolling on the wet and freezing sidewalk. She pinned me down on my back and awkwardly wrapped a hand around my neck, squeezing tightly. She was strong too, but a rage from deep inside me had boiled over and I was goddamn unstoppable in that moment.

I raised a leg and shoved her off with my knee, sending Brigg sprawling. I stumbled to my feet, ran for her gun, and knocked it from Brigg's hold, as she had only just recovered it. She pushed me off and kicked me so hard in my side that I fell and was left gasping for air.

Brigg bent down and picked up her pistol once more. She stopped directly over me and aimed point-blank. "I'm so sorry, Mr. Snow."

One crack and then another rang through the air.

I froze, waiting for the pain—waiting to stop breathing....

Brigg's legs buckled and she toppled backward onto the ground. Her gun fell free from her hold as she let out a sharp, agonizing cry of pain.

I took a small breath and struggled into a sitting position to look at her.

Someone had shot her in the kneecaps.

I slowly looked behind me.

Calvin lowered his aim and slid his pistol back into his holster before running toward us. He crouched to retrieve Brigg's weapon first, tucking it in the back of his pants, before bending down and hoisting me to my feet. He wrapped his arms around me and I began to cry in absolute and utter relief.

I was freezing and soaking wet.

But alive in Calvin's arms.

Sirens and the wail of an ambulance echoed in the immediate vicinity.

Calvin pulled back to hold my face, kissing me over and over. "I love you. I love you so much, Sebastian."

I nodded. I couldn't say anything. I just kept crying and trying to smile.

Behind Calvin, Neil was back on his feet, holding his side.

"Neil?" I finally croaked.

He held his hand up. "Just a graze. You okay?"

"Y-yeah. I—thank you."

He only nodded.

I smiled before hugging Calvin again.

I was really okay.

Brigg lived to see another day.

Not that I imagined she'd enjoy how the rest of her life was going to play out.

And it turned out, I owed Neil.

A lot.

The morning of Valentine's Day when he approached me at the Emporium, Neil had been wasted. He wasn't handling seeing me again so well, especially not with Calvin around at the same time. He'd been drinking and said a lot of things he later regretted.

He'd followed Brigg in his car when he overheard me asking for a ride to Calvin's precinct. He told me that he had intended on giving me a bit more of his mind. It was only when Brigg didn't go to the precinct, Neil said something inside him sobered up. He didn't know what was happening but could only think to tell Calvin where I was being driven.

If he hadn't been drunk when he shot Brigg and saved my head from being blown to pieces, she'd likely be deader than a doornail.

And Neil didn't want me back, which was more than fine by me. He was angry, bitter, violent, and in need of help—but what mattered was that Neil was innocent.

Calvin and Quinn told me I hadn't been alone in the belief that he'd been involved, but it didn't make me feel better. Neil had once been someone I cared for—and then to believe him able to commit such horror….

All I could do was apologize and hope… someday he'd find his own happy ending.

"This one is nice," Max said. He turned his laptop on the table toward me to point at an apartment for rent. "It has a fireplace. That's pretty fancy."

It had been about two weeks. I was still living at Pop's, but not having my own place was making me climb the walls, so Max had come over on our joint Monday off to help with my new humble abode search.

I frowned. "No laundry in building."

"You're making this impossible," he said, turning the computer back to him. "Laundry in building, walk-up, no ground floor apartment—there's nothing listed at the price you want."

"My old place was rent-controlled," I protested.

"Look at something outside of the Village."

"It has to be walking distance to the Emporium."

Max growled. "Dude, just get a cot and move in there, then."

"I'm almost at that point—don't joke."

"I thought you loved your dad?"

"I do. But you try being thirty-three and needy for your guy, only to be cockblocked by your charming father at every turn. I can't be thrown up against the fridge and properly manhandled when my dad is constantly a room away."

"Please stop, this is too much information," Max begged.

"Well, now you understand how important this apartment is."

Max grumbled something under his breath and started clicking away again.

"Thanks for helping me," I added.

"Yeah, yeah. You know I love you, even if you're a pain."

"Now you're going to make me blush."

A bark on the stairs indicated that Pop and Maggie were back from their outing.

I glanced up when the front door opened. "Hey, Dad."

"Hey you two," he called cheerfully while taking Maggie's leash off. "Kiddo, Calvin is downstairs. He asked me to send you outside."

I perked up. "He doesn't want to come in?"

Pop shrugged, busying himself with his winter clothes.

"Er—all right." I stood. "I'll be right back, Max."

"No problem. I'll just be here, searching for an apartment that exists only in your deepest fantasies."

"Keep up the good work." I tugged one of my new sweaters on as I left the apartment and headed down the stairs. I pushed the building's front door open, pausing at the sight of my ever-gorgeous boyfriend. "Cal? What're you...."

There was a dog on a leash at his side.

No special breed, just a cute-as-hell mutt with a big puppy grin on his face.

Calvin looked down at the dog and then back at me. "Dillon," he stated. "That's what the shelter called him, anyway."

I gave him a look as I walked forward. "Go on," I prodded. I felt myself smiling, but tried to keep my happiness contained long enough for Calvin to properly explain.

Calvin reached out for my hand. "I'm not... ready for something like an official service dog. It's too—real for me." He tightened his hold. "But... I met with a doctor."

Unexpected. "You did?"

He looked down at Dillon briefly before meeting my gaze again. "She said I have PTSD."

I nodded.

"*Surprise*," he said quietly. "I'm not... sure I'll go back. At least right away. But...."

Calvin trailed off and I tightened my hold on his hand once more. "But?" I nudged.

"I told her that I only have one goal. To get better for you." Calvin stared at me before tugging me a bit closer. "Because I want to be the sort of man you deserve."

"You already—" Him shaking his head cut me off.

"I know that I'm not okay," Calvin said. "And I love you too much to let that hurt you. So I need to get better."

I glanced at Dillon, who cocked his head to one side and wagged his tail against the sidewalk. Reaching out, I pet the dog's head before saying, "Get better for *us*. Because we're in this together. Aren't we?"

And thank God—Calvin smiled. "Yeah, we are."

"So, where's Dillon from, if not the K4V program?" I asked, crouching down to rub the dog's face.

"One of your father's shelters—Puppy Pals. William helped pick him out."

I looked back up. So Pop calling in a favor a few weeks back…. He'd been planning to talk to Calvin himself about getting a dog?

"You talked to my dad and not me?"

"Don't be upset."

"No. I'm not." I honestly wasn't. So long as Calvin was talking to *someone*, that's all that mattered. And if it took first a doctor and my father before he had the courage to come to me, so be it. I'd wait forever for Calvin. I just wanted him to feel safe and happy.

Calvin cleared his throat. "I've also been thinking about that mailbox."

I immediately looked up again before standing. "Really?"

"Really," Calvin agreed. He smiled widely, and I swear his beautiful gray eyes twinkled. "I've always liked ampersands."

Sebastian Snow and Calvin Winter return in:

The Mystery of the Moving Image
(Snow & Winter: Book Three)

C.S. Poe is a Lambda Literary and two-time EPIC award finalist, and a FAPA award-winning author of gay mystery, romance, and speculative fiction. She resides in New York City, but has also called Key West and Ibaraki, Japan home in the past. She has an affinity for all things cute and colorful and a major weakness for toys. C.S. is an avid fan of coffee, reading, and cats. She's rescued two cats—Milo and Kasper do their best on a daily basis to distract her from work.

C.S. is an alumna of the School of Visual Arts.

Her debut novel, *The Mystery of Nevermore*, was published 2016.

cspoe.com

ALSO BY C.S. POE

SERIES:
Snow & Winter
The Mystery of Nevermore
The Mystery of the Curiosities
The Mystery of the Moving Image
The Mystery of the Bones

A Lancaster Story
Joy
Kneading You
Color of You

The Silver Screen
Lights. Camera. Murder.

NOVELS:
Southernmost Murder

NOVELLAS
11:59

SHORT STORIES:
Love in 24 Frames
That Turtle Story
New Game, Start
Love, Marriage, and a Baby Carriage
Love Has No Expiration

Visit cspoe.com for free slice-of-life codas, titles in audio, and available foreign translations.

Join C.S. Poe's mailing list to stay updated on upcoming releases, sales, conventions, and more!
bit.ly/CSPoeNewsletter